PANDEMIC LOVE

MACKENZIE MASTERS

FOREWORD

Two broken hearts. Two shattered lives, thrust into the same orbit by circumstance during the Covid-19 lockdown.

Mallory and Andrew had every reason to keep their distance. Once burned, twice shy, in an extraordinary situation where social distancing evaporated any chance of intimacy…until Mal's miracle child brought them together. You'll meet Ed, the billionaire CEO, Mallory's eccentric boss and Andrew's college roommate. And Millie, Mal's confidant who entices her best friend into a world where passion and danger walk hand in hand.

You'll be rooting for Mallory and Andrew as they succumb to one night of passion and then struggle with the magnitude of what that could mean in a pair of broken homes where all relationships come with baggage.

It's a love story for our times that will touch your heart and renew your faith in humanity…and the future.

MacKenzie Masters

CHAPTER ONE

M ALLORY
We made love the night before he left.
It took longer than normal for Ella to go
to sleep. In the three years since she came to us with Down
syndrome, I always considered her a blessing. She didn't
have the frightening physical issues many kids do, but she
had gotten my allergies and often woke up crying. Elliot
wasn't much of a husband, but I appreciated how he tried
to accept our beautiful angel. He joined me at all the
therapy meetings, did a stereotypical male's piss-poor job of
changing poopy diapers and cleaning up puke. And he
paid the bills when what the state provided wasn't enough.

I wasn't the easiest person to live with. I'm a smart-ass
on my best days and a goddess from the seventh circle of
hell on my worst. He could deal with my imperfections.
But ultimately, he couldn't deal with the reality that he and
I had an "imperfect child."

Elliot was always an aggressive lover. We were two
minks in heat. Do minks even go into heat? Or is that just
some other author's description of a scene from a porno-

graphic perversion of some Saturday morning cartoon? That monster-chasing Great Dane getting a hard-on for his master's girlfriend.

Now there's a series I could binge on!

Anyway, that night, Elliot bordered on frenzy. Something was missing. He didn't take the time to enjoy my fragrance. There were none of the explorations that warmed me up. Perhaps he hoped to recapture something we had lost so slowly that it was just now becoming evident. Or was it something else?

When Ella's cries echoed from the baby monitor, he gave it up. There was no conversation when I came back to bed after calming her down. He pretended to be asleep, his back turned away from me. It felt final. I felt fear.

The next morning, Elliot got up first. The bastard must have had a bag packed. I learned later that he already had a plan-b. He had left a note.

Mal,

I can't do this. I love you both, but I don't have the emotional fortitude for the day-to-day, for the lifelong commitment. I can't be happy in this situation, and I don't want my frustrations to spill over and damage you and Ella.

I'll give you whatever you ask for in the divorce.

I'm sorry about my own imperfections.

Now you don't have to endure them anymore.

Elliot.

―――――

ANDREW

We made love the night before she left.

With teenage girls in the house, you're supposed to keep the noise down. They are always listening.

And they take notes. I've read them.

Patty liked "high energy" sex. My preference for the tender approach didn't fill her cup.

"I don't care if the girls hear us tonight. I want to ride you like a stallion and scream like a banshee."

I thought I was the stallion and she was the mare. Patty was never very good with sexual metaphors.

I let her. The girls would definitely chide us. I worried about the neighbors. It was as if my body was a conduit to a different place. A different person.

I was right.

She took on another lover. The girls told me later that it had been going on for over a year. I focused on being a good provider and an engaged dad. I had missed the signs.

She beat me out of bed the next morning, bound for the gym, before I stumbled into the kitchen to make breakfast. She had left a note.

Andy,

I'm sorry to tell you this in such a cold and heartless manner. Leaving you this note is the only way I can get through it.

The love I thought would last a lifetime died some time ago. I'm sure you know. You are too good a person to call me on it.

I'm in love with another man. There it is. I've said it. I want to be with him and not with you.

But I also want our girls.

I won't contest anything in our divorce if you give me custody and the house. I have my career and resources. You will need yours to start a fresh life. I hope you find love again like I have.

Thank you for giving me our two beautiful ladies. I'll always honor you for that.

I wish you the happiness you deserve.

Patty.

CHAPTER TWO

MALLORY

When the shit hits the fan, you call your best friend.

Millie was at my house in a heartbeat. Kidless and already an experienced divorcee, she didn't hesitate to unleash her fury on my soon-to-be-ex.

"I never liked that guy, Mal. And ever since he got the stadium deal and became 'king shit' in the construction contractor world, he's been more interested in himself than in anybody else."

"If you didn't like him, why didn't you tell me before I married him?"

"Remember? I was married, too, back then. We were all about security and hunks in those days."

A warm memory of Millie's bad influence on me at college bubbled up. Our carefree coital adventures could have been fodder for a series of steamy porn films.

"We both latched on to these handsome alpha males who did well financially. By the time you were ready to

4

walk down the aisle, I was already beginning to realize that money and sex weren't enough to sustain a marriage."

"Yeah," I said. "And I probably wouldn't have listened to you if you had warned me."

Millie bounced my two-year-old on her knee. Elise giggled and grinned. I hoped she was still young enough not to miss her father.

"I refuse to believe that this little angel was the kicker for Elliot's exit," Millie said. "She's not imperfect at all. In fact, she's better than perfect."

"I'm grateful to have my own income, Mil. Elliot says he'll pay child support, but we need every penny to cover her therapy and early intervention stuff."

"What do you think your boss will say about the divorce?"

"Ed? As long as it doesn't impact the business, he probably won't even notice. That guy's ADD is off the chart. It's made him rich, but he can't even focus on a dumpster fire for more than a few minutes."

"That's one good thing, Mal. You're his grounding force and he knows it. Right brain crazies require discipline. He needs a dominatrix."

"You know the first commandment of leadership, Mil."

"Nope. I follow very few commandments."

"Thou shalt not put thy rod in thy staff."

"So," I continued, "what's it like being single in your thirties, Millie? Do I ever have a chance of getting laid by a decent male again?"

Millie gave me one of her "are you nuts?" looks. "With your body? You'll be peeling them off you like flies on picnic potato salad."

"I'm talking about love, Mil. Will I ever find it?"

———

ANDREW

Eddie may have had a huge blind spot for the emotional needs of others, but we were instantly there for one another in times of true crisis.

The moment I told him Patty had left me, I could feel the focus.

"That sucks, pal. I'm canceling everything tonight. Come on over to the house at seven. "

True to his word, my best friend left his cell phone on the charger. The screens that constantly blared Bloomberg in every room in the house were dark. He met me at the door with a vodka bottle, ice bucket, and two glasses in hand.

"Enter, old buddy. Let's medicate and you can tell me all about it."

For a world-class entrepreneur with his head totally in business, I was surprised to discover how aware Eddie was about my situation.

"Yeah," he said as we sat in the living room of his expansive mansion, "I hate to say it, but I could see that one coming a mile away. We didn't stop to think that the kind of girls who were screwing us like rabbits in school might not be wired for commitment. Patty always had a wanderlust. I worried that a stable guy like you might be too boring for her."

I struggled to believe that. "Too boring? We've been around the world. I've given her every material thing she asked for from a Lexus SUV to her dream house."

"And," Eddie added, "a set of world-class boobs. That was the red flag. It was totally her ask. You loved her just as she was."

I sucked down the double vodka and held out my glass for a refill. "You know, for a guy with the attention span of a gnat, you're about the most attentive friend I could imagine."

"Shit," Eddie said, deflecting the compliment, "if I were a diamond, I'd have so many flaws that no jeweler would touch me. Why do you think I'm still single after putting all these stupid financial points on the board? I should be fucking Kim Kardashian. I'm up there with Musk and Zuck and I couldn't sustain a relationship if the stock price depended on it."

"What do I do, partner?" I asked. "I'll probably get my girls on weekends, but as far as other women are concerned, I'm damaged goods now."

"Far from it. Healing takes time, and I know a ton of guys who needed a mulligan before hitting a hole in one. Focus on your business. You're the best human resource and biz ops consultant on the planet. Throw yourself into that world until you can re-center. And keep seeing your shrink. I've paid for a new wing on my psychiatrist's house by now."

"You mean you can concentrate for a full hour?"

"She's like a Catholic school nun—hits me with a ruler if I finger my cell phone during a session."

"That's good advice. My therapist is the only other voice besides yours who warned me that something like this might happen."

Eddie took a sip of his drink. "It may take a while, but don't be afraid to risk a bedroom encounter or two after you get your feet under you. Nothing restores your self-confidence like a beautiful woman screaming your name while riding you like a mechanical bull at a country bar."

"That's a picture I can't visualize right now, my friend. But it sure would be nice to wake up with a warm female body next to mine at some point."

"You're a good man, Andrew," Eddie said. "Karma ultimately prevails. Patty's departure will be a good thing in the long run. And I believe the love of your life is out there, perhaps closer than you realize."

I took another dose of my drink. "For both of us, Eddie. I definitely don't want to be sitting here, drinking myself blind with you when I'm sixty-four."

"Oh, we'll be doing that anyway, Andy. Paul McCartney be damned."

CHAPTER THREE

TWO YEARS LATER...

MALLORY

The pandemic changed everything. The shift was palpable, monumental. Life became divided into two eras: everything that came before Corona and all that happened after.

Elliot honored his word. I had my human resources career, but with a special needs kid, his alimony and child support were crucial.

And he had re-married. "Angel" gave him that perfect baby he couldn't get with me. Wife number two was watching her man closely and expected him to take the high road.

Guilt is a wonderful thing.

In the two years since my husband left, his disconnection from our lives became inversely proportional to my love affair with Mr. Hitachi and Duracell batteries.

I joined the "Dildo of the Month Club" and gave each of my new friends names like King, Ludlum, and Grisham. Some girls fantasize about rock stars; I prefer authors.

We continued going together to Ella's therapy and evaluations for a time. Then he started making excuses. Except for the direct deposits, there had been no contact with my ex in ten months.

The pandemic played a role. I'm sure Elliot worried about how his business would sustain the economic impact.

Our company stood at a crossroads, too.

Working from home became crucial. Ella's daycare was closed. My parents lived a thousand miles away. Everyone else focused on survival. I was on my own.

People think a good human resource person shows compassion for employees. That's bullshit. We're there for one reason—to protect the company from lawsuits. I can smile, blink my fake eyelashes, and make anybody feel "valued." If there was an Academy of Human Resource Arts and Sciences, I would surely win Miss Congeniality.

My only real concern was how to keep my own paychecks coming.

Furloughs were on the way. I helped our CEO identify essential workers. We developed a game plan that would save our company money but still let us fund health care benefits…for now. The work involved in downsizing a worldwide workforce turned out to be immense. We hired an outside firm to help us with the burden. Today, I would see who they had assigned to us. I hoped the person came with some skills.

———

ANDREW

Zoom meetings sucked. But they are the only option when you couldn't travel and your customers were all bunkered down at home. Since I owned the firm, I got to choose my key clients. I took this project because they were local and the gig could keep the cash flowing my way for at least a year.

Ed and I were friends, too. That didn't hurt. The CEO was my college classmate. We knew each other's embarrassing secrets, shared common conquests, and had enough dirt on one another to sink four careers.

So naturally, Ed tried to recruit me when he went public. We both were smart enough to realize how friendships could crater if we worked too closely.

And by then, the fruits of my own labors were abundant. We decided it would better serve our friendship to maintain a little "social distance."

Three of us entered the video conference room: Ed, me, and his HR VP. I was aware of her reputation. We had talked peripherally over the years. I would find out how good she really was now.

———

MALLORY

Ed kicked things off. "Andy! Great to see your ugly face. And thanks for helping Mal and me out with this inconvenience. I've always kept senior support staff thin, and you'll add enormous value."

Andrew had his pandemic vibe going on. His dark-brown hair curled at the edges. I guessed he did a little more than the usual preparation for the meeting. A manicured mustache and goatee ran between the dimples of what had once been a clean-shaven face. The pattern of wrinkles on his polo shirt told me it was a recent acquisition, probably fresh out of the LL Bean bag.

What little I could see of his upper body gave me tingles. I resolved to break my author requirement and name my next dildo of the month after him.

"I read Mallory's plan, partner," Andrew said. His voice was deeper and softer than I remembered. The gentle smile made me wonder what could have possessed his ex to start fucking another guy.

"It's in line with what my other clients are doing. You're very generous. The communications are buttoned-down, and I think the timeline for execution will give the team enough runway to digest and adjust. Excellent job all around!"

Ed's eyes diverted, as usual, to his smartphone. The king of multi-tasking and the Don of delegation had a distraction.

"Hey guys, I have to take this call. Go forth and do things. Tell me what help you need from me."

Ed's screen disappeared. Andrew and I were "virtually" alone.

———

ANDREW

I have a horrible memory. I write down the important stuff. This is what I wrote about Mallory:

"Mallory Mason-Michaels: thirty-two, divorced. Gemini. Daughter–age five. BA/MBA in Human Resources. Started with Ed out of college and rose to HR VP in less than ten years. Able administrator. Yoga, dancing, smart (ass), impatient."

What I didn't write down was how I wanted to know what those delectable lips tasted like and how just imagining what might be underneath the pressing contours of her conservative button-down top gave my cock a mind of its own.

I wondered what her notebook said about me. Thirty-seven, divorced, no life about covering it.

"I'm glad we're working together, Andrew." I focused on her voice. Vice Presidential, confident, perhaps a little brash. Women needed to over-compensate with so many stupid men still judging them. "How is the work-from-home thing going?"

I thought about the backdrop she must see behind me. I bought a place big enough to accommodate my teenagers on weekends. I got the pool so they would want to party here instead of with their friends. And I thought they enjoyed being able to escape to Dad's house when Mom and husband number two got too intense.

"I moved here after Patty left. It's much more than I need. But it's a magnet for my girls. Wanted them to have some reason to want to hang out with boring Dad."

"Where did you end up?"

"Yale Meadows. I bought on Sunderland Street."

A strange expression broke through Mallory's mask. "Ella and I are on Sunderland. What's the address?"

"9125."

"You're less than a block away. I'm surprised I haven't seen you at the park."

"Teenagers aren't into the park so much anymore. They would rather get skin cancer lying around the pool. I'm glad they seem to prefer my chlorinated water to their mother's."

Mallory kept digging. I didn't think either of us wanted to tell six hundred people they were losing their jobs. "How has it been? Not just the pandemic life, but the single life?"

"Not much of a life. Nobody's doing anything face to face these days. And I imagine both of our careers are consuming well over forty hours a week right now. How are you navigating the work thing with a five-year-old in tow?"

"Ella is independent. I don't enjoy sticking her in front of the screen all day. About a month ago, I found a babysitter. One of her therapists is off for the summer. She agreed to stick to my lockdown protocols. She hangs with Ella on weekdays. It's like having a full-time teacher at home."

Are there any men in your life? Are you as horny as I am? Would your daughter sleep through a one-night stand of screaming, passionate sex?

Then out loud, I said, "That's great! The biggest challenge I have is keeping the girls in masks and away from large gatherings. They still think they're immortal."

Stomping my libido devil back into its cage, the good fairy who remained liked this conversation. Perhaps we both appreciated having someone we could talk to like this.

Mallory's hair had grown during the lockdown. She must have been a natural dishwater blonde. Patty's stylist bills told me that maintaining a look contrary to nature's way required both time and money. Mallory was also sparse in the make-up department. A little color on the cheeks and just enough foundation to dim the freckles.

I wondered what she looked like without it, naked and writhing under me on a mattress. Hell, I'd settle for a garage floor or the back seat of a Volkswagen at this point.

"I don't look forward to the teenage years," she said. "I wonder what Ella will be like then. Sometimes, I wish she would never grow older than she is now."

I could relate. "I remember those days. Nothing can beat that tiny warm body snuggling up next to you before bed. You are the most important person on the planet, the one they want hugging them when they hurt and the smile that lights them up at the start of each day."

Mallory glanced away from the screen. I guessed she was checking the clock. How much more time could she spare? "How are you holding up, really, Andrew? Ed says no husband loved his wife more deeply." Her eyes darted for a second, as if she thought she might have ventured too far out of bounds. "I guess that's a personal question. You don't have to answer it."

I thought about it a lot. But that was the first time anybody had encouraged me to put it into words.

———

MALLORY

Where did that come from? Shut up with the personal questions, Mallory. Andrew is a vendor and one of Ed's best friends. You just jumped way over the line.

I intended to reel things back in when I saw his eyes lose focus. His face reflected the essence of resignation, sadness, and perhaps some acceptance. I could relate. I felt the embarrassing discharge that always gave away my emotions start to dampen my panties.

Dammit. I'd have to wash a load of whites if this kept up.

"I miss her warmth next to me at night, Mal." He shortened my name. That was new. "I miss calling her up and having her meet me for dinner someplace on the spur of the moment. I miss the two of us holding hands when the girls have a concert or a sports thing. I miss sending her flowers for no reason. Most of all, I miss the pillow talk. This may be TMI—and tell me if it is—but I loved that most of all. Our conversations weren't that deep. She was never a very thoughtful person. But just knowing that I had a listener meant the world to me. Sometimes I would babble for twenty minutes straight. I knew she couldn't have cared less. She was present, and that was enough. At least I thought it was then."

I got it. How I longed for adult conversation, for the smell of a man's body pressed against my own, for the sex. Perhaps I wouldn't wait for that next shipment. I had a really cool rechargeable tickler that I could rechristen in Andrew's honor tonight.

Okay, calm down, Mal. Save that one for your shrink.

"I understand," I said. "I love Ella, but what I wouldn't give for someone who speaks in more than just a few syllables."

Andrew's eyes focused on me. It was like he was trying to read me in the pixels of his monitor. We were less than a block away from one another. It might as well have been a million miles.

"Let's adult on this communication plan," he said. Back to business. The connection broke. For a few moments, I had been whole again. The emptiness returned.

CHAPTER FOUR

A NDREW
"When Mallory told me we were neighbors, my heart jumped. I don't know why it did that."

My psychiatrist had her head in her notebook. She still wrote things down. It was one of the few face-to-face appointments I kept. We didn't wear masks. She kept her distance, both physical and professional.

"You're lonely. That's normal for someone who was married for seventeen years. Are you attracted to her?"

I could feel the twitch beneath my belt buckle. It was familiar, exciting, a little frightening. The doc sensed it. She never asked questions without already knowing the answers.

"I'll mark that as a 'yes,'" she said, displaying the half-smile I had a love-hate relationship with.

I repeated what the HR manual said. "It's not a good thing. We're professional colleagues, and she works for my best friend."

"Listen, Andrew. These are extraordinary times. You both are living in extraordinary situations. You don't have the usual support systems and are going it alone on every level. And nothing makes people horny like anxiety. So many of my patients are telling me about their stress fucks these days."

I didn't like the conversation's direction. There is nothing more embarrassing than getting a boner in your lady shrink's office. But my curiosity overcame my discomfort. "Tell me some 'stress fuck' stories," I said.

She looked up from the notebook. "You're avoiding this. But okay, I'll tell you one." The Doc always looked me straight in the eye when she dished out the directions, and I wondered if that was what this was about. "I have a patient about your age. Divorced seven months. He ran into a high school girlfriend at the grocery store. They both wore masks, but the recognition—and the attraction were mutual. She's had four husbands. The last one couldn't handle her drama any better than the first three. But that didn't stop them. They began a brief mating dance via text messaging. One week, he wanted nothing to do with her. The next, they were screwing each other breathless. He knows he can't live with that crazy woman. But they both have needs and decided some stress fucking turned out to be their solution."

She had my attention. "And what did you tell him?"

"That she probably is an STD factory and has Covid-19."

"And his response?"

"His need for physical touch at the moment outstrips his need for a long and productive life. That happens. Sometimes you just roll the dice. There are consequences either way. Don't do it and you crater psychologically. Do it and you may die. Neither outcome is ideal."

Death was a pretty final outcome. I was totally confused. "So, what are you telling me?"

"It's okay to explore and see where this goes. You are a well-adjusted, self-actualized human being, thrust into a situation that nobody ought to have to endure. Just understand that whatever you do comes with its own shit. Be prepared to deal with it."

"As in my best friend finding out that I'm spending time with his employee?"

"He won't care about that as long as it doesn't affect him. I'm talking about taking on the responsibility of a relationship. The question you have to ask yourself is, 'Am I ready for that?'"

————

MALLORY

It was after five. The babysitter had left. I was thinking about dinner when I heard Ella scream. There was a red mark on her thigh. Some sort of bite. A distant memory said spider. I didn't know if her allergies extended to insects, but her pediatrician said not to fool around with bug bites. Get her to a hospital.

I needed backup so I could be in the rear seat next to her. Nobody answered my agitated calls. I remembered the conversation with Andrew. He was close. I dialed his number. Any port in a storm.

"I'll be right there."

Just hearing his calm voice took the tension down several notches. Seeing him gave me hope.

"I'll drive your car," he said, pressing the front seat as far back as it would go. "You stay next to Ella."

Andrew wore cargo shorts, a T-shirt, and flip-flops. Pool attire. I wondered what that body looked like naked. I shook my head to press the thought back into my subconscious. My daughter's in physical danger and I'm thinking about getting laid. Pretty damn shallow.

"Let's have a peek at that leg, shortcake," Andrew said as he ran a red light right before turning onto the beltway. He snaked an arm toward my screaming child in the car seat, framing the wound in a half-moon circle he made with his thumb and index finger. "Ahh. Yes. Spider bite. I remember those." Andrew looked at Ella through the rearview mirror. But he was talking to me. "If there were allergies, you would already be as big as a balloon, baby. Tell Mom to get an EpiPen from the doctor, just in case you need one later. But in my unprofessional opinion, I think you will be okay."

He was soothing me, but he was speeding. The situation worried the guy. He just didn't want us to know it.

And his assessment turned out to be on the money. The ER folks confirmed the spider bite. They gave us instructions on how to keep it clean and a prescription for an EpiPen and some antihistamines in case of complications.

"You're two lucky parents," the doctor said. "Your daughter is one healthy girl, better than many kids I see with Down syndrome. Watch out. She will be a handful when she gets stronger." She shot a smile at Andrew that made me jealous. "And she has your blue eyes, Dad. Ella will be a heartbreaker."

Andrew blushed. The doctor vanished into the hallways but not before giving him that "I would totally fuck you if you asked," look. I wanted to tell her that this man wasn't my husband.

I suddenly wished he were.

Andrew smiled at me. "Let's figure out dinner, Mom."

———

ANDREW

I texted the girls. They were hanging at the pool and needed something to do. I had them order up some take-out. They met us in Mallory's driveway. Since I didn't know what the likes or limitations might be, I ordered a broad selection, from salads and fruit to chicken piccata and pasta.

Dani, my oldest, scooped Ella out of her mother's arms. "You're cute! And I bet you're hungry as a bear." Mallory's kid had a new best friend.

Dana, the one with the homemaker skills and the asthma, set up the spread. I could see the stresses of the day lift from Mallory's shoulders as Dana pressed a wine glass into her hands. "Drink this," my baby girl directed. "Doctor Dana's orders."

"Four to one," I said as we all sat around Mallory's dinner table.

Ella repeated everything between bites. "Four one," she said. She waved a hand at Dani. "Again!"

Dani laughed. "Four to one, Ella. We like outnumbering the men."

"So many attractive women and just one man," I added, patting the beautiful baby on the top of her head. "I like those odds."

"You're embarrassing me, Dad," Dani said. "And you're being disrespectful to Miss Mallory."

"Yeah, Dad," Dana added, scooping some pasta into her mouth. "Your jokes aren't funny. Just ask questions and listen."

I looked across the table at our hostesses. Ella happily attacked some more mandarin oranges. "Listen," she said, pointing a half-chewed piece of fruit at me like one of the nuns at my old Catholic grade school.

Today's adventures were past history. Ella's mother

seemed to have recovered, too. She laughed at the exchange.

"It's been a long time since I've had anyone over for dinner. You guys are kind to risk exposure by coming in here."

"We're the ones who are probably exposing you," Dana said, pointing a fork at her sister. "Sexy pants over here has a boyfriend, and I bet they don't wear masks."

Dani blushed, shooting daggers at her sister. "Shut up, Dana. Henry is religious about distancing."

"Henry?" I asked. I was always the last to know about these things. "Who is Henry?"

The girls ignored me.

"Yeah, right," Dana shot back. "As long as you don't define 'face sucking' as a violation."

I looked at Mallory and shrugged. "See what you have ahead of you? You may be glad you only have one set of moods to deal with."

"There wasn't anyone or anything who could keep me from my boyfriend when I was your age, Dani," Mallory said. "I was a poor influence."

There are moments when two women bond. I could see it happening between Dani and Mallory. The two exchanged knowing looks. My oldest never got this backup from her biological mother.

"Dads and sisters don't understand about love," Dani said. "When it happens, you just have to accept it." She looked at Dana and me. The unspoken message: "Mallory gets me. You two don't."

"Okay, face sucker," Dana said, "Let's clean up and let this poor woman and her child recover from having us all descend upon them."

"You don't have to run off," Mallory said. "And please

don't worry about the dishes." She shot a glance at me. I still couldn't decode its meaning. "It's the least I can do."

My girls swept the wreckage off of the table. Dana refilled Mallory's wine glass. "Keep medicating, Miss Mallory. We've got this."

"Dad can stay if he wants," Dani said over her shoulder. "We have to go back to our 'other' home and make sure Mom is behaving."

"And don't forget, Dad," Dana added. "Tomorrow is your custody night." She said the word custody as if it were a disease. "Please think of something fun for us to do together for a change."

CHAPTER FIVE

M ALLORY

He stayed. We talked while his girls cleaned things up. He sat on the edge of the tub and listen to me babble about work as I gave Ella a bath. And when I got a call from Ed to handle an employee issue, he read to my daughter while I sorted out the latest drama. It took longer than I expected. Darkness had fallen when I finally looked up from my laptop screen.

Ella lay passed out against Andrew's ribs. Her tiny hand held his. I was instantly horny.

"Want me to relieve you of that extra weight?" I whispered.

Andrew looked content. "No hurry. It's bringing back happy memories."

"Thank you for today," I said. "There are moments when I really miss having a husband."

Dammit. I did it again. He didn't need to hear that. I was probably triggering his sadness and shame with my own.

"There are moments when I miss 'being' a husband," he murmured.

I gently lifted Ella into my arms. She flopped onto my shoulder like a rag doll, sound asleep.

Andrew stood. "I'll let you have your quality time," he said.

The quality time I wanted was with him. "At least let me buy you one more glass of wine before you go. If you don't mind waiting a few minutes for me to get the munchkin settled."

Andrew nodded. He patted Ella's head. "Sleep well, shortcake. You've got a great mom."

———

I PRAYED THAT TUCKING MY BABY IN WOULDN'T awaken her. Seventy percent of the time, it did, and I would have to rock her back to sleep. Andrew must have had the magic touch. Ella coiled into a ball as I covered her up, a contented smile spreading across her face.

"Daddy," she whispered.

That just about destroyed me. The one thing I wanted desperately to give my daughter was beyond my reach.

I swallowed the tears. A man sat in my living room for the first time in months.

When I tiptoed back, he had wine glasses prepared. Andrew stood by the fireplace, holding two bottles. "More red, or would you like to shift gears to the white?"

My head was screaming, Screw the wine, buster. I'd rather screw you instead.

"I love the Meiomi," I said.

"I thought so." Andrew poured for us. "There's a lot in the pantry. You must have the city's largest supply of disinfectant wipes, too."

I raised a toast. "On sale at Costco. Who knows how long this lockdown will last!"

"To survival," Andrew said.

"With gratitude," I added.

Andrew's outfit was casual, comfortable, and flattering to his physique. Why would a woman abandon something that attractive? I did a quick scan of my body. My yoga practice was now on video. The scale said I added ten pounds since we started working from home. Suddenly self-conscious, I sat, motioning him to join me on the couch. Three feet separated us. His scent was irresistible. His hair was deliciously askew. I wanted to run my hands through it. The blue eyes that attracted the ER doc were warm and welcoming. There didn't seem to be anything hidden behind them.

But I didn't know this man. I had learned from extensive HR experience that some of the worst humans put on the best faces. He was a divorcee, and as delicious as he looked, a break-up takes two to tango. My conflict was genuine. On the one hand, my own split still stung as if I had just read the note. On the other, I wanted to jump on this man, tear his clothes off, and press that chiseled body against my own.

"Whatever is going through your mind is happening at light speed," Andrew said. "Those eyes are darting back and forth like hummingbird wings."

"Too many things to think about," I lied.

Andrew sipped his wine, looking over the top of the glass in a way that made my juices flow. I pulled one of Ella's blankets over my lap to cover the wet spot. "Tell me a few of them," he said. "It's so rare that I have any face-to-face interactions beyond my girls. I miss all the non-verbal stuff."

"Honestly?"

"Honestly."

"It's awkward. We're work colleagues. What I want to say isn't appropriate for that relationship."

Andrew pursed his lips. He looked like a professor processing a student's answer to a deep philosophical question. I wanted to taste those lips.

"Try saying it anyway."

The wine spoke. "I want you to fuck me senseless." I bit my lip after I said it, wishing I could take it back but wanting it to happen.

Andrew leaned back a bit and raised his eyebrows. "Well!" Was it mock surprise or the real thing? "Nobody has said that to me in a very long time."

I stood and started pacing, the stupid kid's blanket with cartoon characters wrapped around my waist like a skirt. Words spilled out of me.

"I shouldn't have said that. This whole thing, the pandemic, people losing their jobs, the divorce, worrying about my kid," I stopped to stare at him again as if my confidence needed a refill. "Loneliness, desire, passion, it's spinning inside me like a blender."

I sat. Closer to him this time. The hair on his knee tickled me. I was barely under control. "And when I tucked Ella in, she smiled at me and said, 'Daddy.' On top of everything, I'm a terrible mom. I can't even keep a family together. I'm sorry. I apologize. Forget I said it. Jesus, I'm embarrassed."

That was when he touched me. Three of his fingers brushed against my cheek. It was electric.

"You're a terrific mom, Mal. And this life we're living isn't easy. We're two broken people trying to figure out a path to happiness in a world turned upside down. Everything you feel is valid. It's normal. It's okay."

That tripped my trigger.

I put my hands behind Andrew's neck and pulled him to me, kissing him with all the latent hunger that had hidden inside of me for so long. He kissed me back. It was delicious, sincere, and erotic. I pushed Andrew flat onto the couch, climbing on top of him as my oral explorations continued. I unbuttoned his shirt. My hands traveled across his chest, looking for any ounce of tension in his pectoral muscles. They were strong and firm but melted into my fingers as I massaged them.

Andrew didn't stop me. But he was not being an aggressor, either. I wondered if he was bracketing exactly what I needed, opening himself up to me so I might have it. I wanted more. I wanted him to take the lead.

"Please make love to me," I begged. "I know I am breaking a half dozen rules, and I'll probably be apologizing to you in the morning, but…"

Andrew covered my mouth with a palm.

"Where's your bedroom?"

As he stood, I could see his thickening interest. The sight made me drop the blanket. Andrew could see the damp circle that was ever-expanding across the front of my pants. I wrapped my heels around his back and my arms around his neck. "It's that way. Can we stop at the bathroom first?"

Talk about how to destroy the moment! "Can I pee?" What a turnoff. I just should have gone for it.

A delightful chuckle rose from Andrew's chest. His smile enveloped me, and we kissed again as he carried me down the hallway. He set me down next to the sink, looking over his shoulder into the darkness. "That way?" he asked, pointing toward the master bedroom.

His cologne was overpowering. His eyes were pulling me in like magnets. I wanted him naked right now. I wanted to jump him right there in the bathroom.

"I'll only be a minute," I whispered.

———

ANDREW

Mallory's silhouette in the doorway was stunning. Her yoga routine enhanced her curves. The fullness of her mother's body sent thunderbolts of lust toward the pulsing protrusion that rose under the bed sheets. *Yeah. I'm talking about my cock. Allow me a little alteration, will ya?* Mallory's hand spread across the space between her legs. A pair of fingers found their way into her folds as her palm started a slow, circular motion of arousal.

"Get rid of that sheet and let me look at you." Her voice was somewhere between a begging whimper and a command. It added more blood to my presentation.

I pulled the bedclothes aside and lay revealed to her. I thought of a line from my girls' favorite movie.

"As you wish."

"I don't really know anything about you," she said, a note of practiced apology in her voice that I knew was an act. She removed her hand from her warmth and approached me. "Does this make you uncomfortable? No, you've got the biggest erection I've ever seen, so you must want this as bad as I do. But I want you to know that I'm not some street slut who jumps into bed with any guy who saves my kid's life. It's been *so* long, and I have a box full of dildos over there with more mileage on them than a twenty-year-old school bus. But truly…I've admired your work, and that combination of an amazing mind and a beautiful body is what is turning me on. I.."

I put a hand over her mouth. "Mal. It's okay. Fuck me."

She was beside me now. I could sense the sweetness of

the juices on her hand. I took it into my own, sucking on her two drenched fingers as I rolled onto my back.

"Jesus Christ and his all-girl orchestra," Mal moaned. "If you're not inside me in the next ten seconds, I'll cram Patterson and Chandler and Clive into my pussy at the same time and turn the batteries on full."

"Clive?" I asked.

"I have a thing for authors," Mal mumbled, circling her clit until her fingers were a blur. "I name my dildos after them."

"Maybe later," I said. "That would be an interesting sight. But let's see how we fit first." I gripped the throbbing center of her attention with my fist.

Mallory straddled me. Her thighs contracted as she lowered herself onto my cock. It had been a long time for both of us. The simple act of entering her sent a shiver throughout Mallory's body. Her groan vibrated in time.

"Holy mother of George Washington," she whispered. "I can't believe I just came."

"So you're into fantasizing about historical figures, too?" I wondered. "What about Grover Cleveland?"

"Shut the fuck up, Andrew."

Mallory's hands clung to my torso, and she flexed her leg muscles. Measured in and out movements massaged me. With each press, her inner grip tightened around me. "They teach us this move in yoga class. The practice has many applications. I like this one the best."

"How about the Dalai Lama?" I pressed. "Would you do it with him?"

I was trying to distract myself from coming. Mallory began a grind that made her exquisite tits swing in circles. "Knock it off, buster, or I'll shove Robert Ludlum up your ass."

I resolved to send flowers to her yoga teacher. Come to

think of it, I probably would have fucked her yoga teacher, any teacher, any female at that moment.

I pressed upward to meet her in time with her powerful undulations. Whatever skills she may have had before were still in peak form. With gaining confidence, she increased the pace.

"Watch me take you over the finish line," she purred. Just saying it made her peak again. The shudder was an incredible turn-on.

Then we heard the baby monitor.

———

ELLA WAS AWAKE. SHE WASN'T CRYING YET, BUT I KNEW from experience what was coming. Mallory put her fists against her temples and swallowed a frustrated wail. "Not now, Ella. Please! Not now!"

I put my hands behind Mallory's back and guided her body toward me until my arms could encircle her. Mallory's inner muscles still clinched me with fury. "I want to make you come!" she said, tears rolling down her face and onto my chest.

"You will," I said. "Be patient."

———

MALLORY

Then Andrew did an incredible thing. He rolled me onto my side, pulled on his shorts, and flicked my nose with a finger.

"I'll be back."

Moments later, I saw him in the night vision of the baby monitor. He took Ella into his arms and sank back into the overstuffed rocking chair I kept next to her bed. "It's okay, shortcake; tell me about that nasty dream."

Ella melted into his embrace. She still speaks a language of her own, but Andrew seemed to understand every word.

"You're not alone, baby. You're never alone. Your mom is always right here. She always will be. Now you need to rest so you can have a marvelous day tomorrow."

Ella's hand went for Andrew's fingers. Her voice fell to a whisper. Soon her regular breathing told me she was asleep. Andrew returned my miracle girl to her bed, swaddling her in a way that made it feel like his arms were still around her. I made a mental note to steal the idea.

Now Andrew stood in the doorway. His shorts hung by two fingers over the back of his shoulder.

"I enjoyed that intermission," he said, tossing the pants into a corner and walking toward me. "Ella is amazing. I could fall in love with her."

I couldn't take my eyes off him. He noticed.

"Did you cheat on me with any authors while I was gone?"

I giggled. "You wrote a book, Andrew. I read it. 'Strategies for Effective Union Negotiations.' It made me wet."

I sat on the edge of the bed. He stood next to me. The instrument of my ecstasy was at eye level.

His voice was low and oh, so sexy. "Patty was into vibrators for a while. One of the lithium batteries exploded and nearly burned the house down."

"I love it when you talk dirty like that, handsome." I closed my eyes, encircling my breasts with my hands. I squeezed them together, tweaking my nipples as I moaned. They responded, flowering into a pair of erect needlepoints. Andrew responded, too.

"And perhaps another taste," I said, sliding my two

fingers inside of the warm wetness he had so recently enjoyed. It was my turn to savor the flavor. I sucked off the honey, making noises that I saw were getting the job done.

In another moment, Andrew stood at full attention.

"I would love to take care of you with my tongue," I said, leaning toward my target. I dipped my fingers inside of me again, applying the natural lubrication to Andrew's beautiful, thick cock.

Andrew cradled my head in his hands, tilting me up as he bent down to kiss me. The improv comedy performance was over. Time for the love story.

"We have all night."

He pressed me to the mattress, spreading my legs with his knees. Soft sounds of my baby's breath whispered from the monitor. Andrew's throbbing magnificence entered me. He nibbled my neck until he found the right spot. I responded with a groan. He circled it with his tongue. I made a note to guide that incredible patois southward later on. Andrew began his soft rhythm. And I came again like a rocket.

CHAPTER SIX

MALLORY
We did it all. Four hours' worth. It didn't even begin to unpack everything I still held inside of me. That didn't matter. Having this incredible man make love to me was exquisite. And satisfying him did wonders for my self-esteem.

When we finished, we showered together. It was a mindfulness exercise—luxurious, sensitive, and poignant. I could sense Andrew recalling moments with his ex as we massaged one another with shower gel. He allowed me the same journey. We weren't surrogates. All love is built on past love. We both wanted to assuage our battle scars. We both wanted to help each other begin to heal. Selfless self-ishness at its best.

At least, that was how I was rationalizing it at the moment. In reality, I was so damn turned on and needy that I would have fallen for anything male with two legs and a penis.

Then the pillow talk began. I told Andrew about Elliot, about my college debauchery, about how hard it was to find good medical care for my daughter, about the act I had perfected that made me successful in business, and about the scared little girl that still lived at the center of my soul. We conversed for the next two hours until our eyes drooped and words slurred into a deep, calming sleep, the first restful sleep I had enjoyed in years.

Such was the depth of my slumber that I didn't realize we had company until the sun rays tickled my face around seven in the morning.

Ella lay between us. She must have stirred, and Andrew brought her to our bed without awakening me. She lay sandwiched between our backs, a broad smile bent upward below her slumbering eyes. Her arms tried to circle Andrew's torso.

Peacefulness personified.

———

ANDREW

What Mallory didn't know was that Ella woke me around five. I heard movement on the monitor and went into her bedroom to check it out.

"Potty," she said with a grin.

I knew the drill. She read to me from her favorite book as she took care of business.

"Hungry?" I asked.

Ella nodded. She knew where her breakfast provisions were. We talked for almost an hour as she ate, in the unique language of a kid learning to speak "on the scenic route."

I felt gratitude for my two girls. But this amazing spirit who was living life at her own pace and in her own way touched my heart. I could learn something from her.

When Ella finished eating, she pointed toward the bedroom. "Mommy," she said. "Snuggle."

A brilliant suggestion. I realized that it was Saturday. I had work to do, but it could wait. I loaded Mallory's daughter onto my back, and we snuck back into the bedroom.

Ten minutes later, all three of us were sleeping again.

————

MALLORY

I slid out from under the warmth of the covers. For the first time in months, I could take a shower without worrying about my kid. The hand-washed dishes in the sink told me the story of Andrew and Ella's breakfast date. I thought about my to-do list. I knew Andrew would want to get back to his own in-box soon.

A sea of conflicting emotions filled my head. The tingle between my legs was a reminder of the unforgettable events of the previous night. I couldn't remember any experience that came close. Andrew personified everything missing from my marriage to Elliot. I wanted him with every fiber of my being.

But my shattered heart warned me to be wary. There was still so much we didn't know about one another. I couldn't fail my daughter again. We would take it slow.

Tiny footsteps announced Ella's arrival. I could hear the shower down the hallway.

"Clean… Privacy," my daughter said.

"Do you like this man?" I asked, sweeping Ella into my arms.

She giggled as we spun around the living room. "Yeah… Snuggle. I like it."

Anytime I got over two words out of her was a victory. Her eyes caught sight of the flat screen. "*Frozen?*"

It was the weekend. Popping on the Disney classic would keep her focused for an hour. I brought the film up On Demand. Cinderella's castle appeared. She was hooked for the hundredth time.

I locked the safety gate and padded toward the master bath.

Andrew was still in the shower when I slipped in, naked behind him.

"Good morning, handsome. Anything you want to share about one of the most exquisite nights of your life?"

Andrew grinned and tweaked my nipple with a thumb and forefinger.

"You fart in your sleep."

CHAPTER SEVEN

A NDREW
Pizza, pop, and a game night earned a four
on a five-point scale from my girls. We stayed up
way too late watching *Ant Man* and *The Wasp*. Dana was in
a full-on Paul Rudd phase. Dani was into Ryan Reynolds,
so *The Proposal* followed. Somewhere in the second act,
they dismissed me, promising to clean up the monumental
mess we had made.

I drifted off to sleep, thinking about Mallory. After
taking each other to the pinnacle of passion, we both barfed
out our tales of woe, talking without filters and listening with
buckets of empathy. It was the best kind of conversation. No
judgment. Only clarifying questions. And round after round
of passionate sex when the stories cut our emotions loose.
There would be lots to talk about with my shrink this week.

The girls decided I needed to wake up around ten on
Sunday morning. They brought me breakfast in bed and
insisted that we all watch *Annie* for the zillionth time. My
frame of reference for audience participation was *The Rocky*

Horror Picture Show. Annie was Patty's contribution to my suffering. Not my favorite film by a mile but required viewing whenever the girls were in the mood to relive the days before the split.

I sat in the center of the king-sized bed, a mop-top planted on each side.

"I like Miss Mallory," Dani said, munching on a slice of raisin toast.

"You like her because she doesn't give you crap about Henry," Dana said.

"Who is Henry?" I repeated my question from Saturday's supper. "Will someone please give me the four one one?"

Dana was happy to oblige. "Dani met Henry at youth group. His dad is the associate pastor. He's a year older and knows how to kiss."

That annoyed my older daughter. "Shut up, Dana."

"Silvia Marshall told me. She knows firsthand."

"Any other dimensions of this gentleman's personality that bear highlighting?" I asked, trying to sound only mildly interested.

Dani dropped her chin onto her palm, closing her eyes to conjure up a memory. "He plays chess!" She sighed. Dani was my intellectual. A hormonal teenage girl with a sharp mind that intimidated the boys.

Dana frowned, a sign that something smartass would soon erupt. "Did you say chess or chest?"

"Fuck off, Dana."

My face darkened. "Where did you learn that language, young lady?"

The two girls dissolved into waves of laughter, the contagious kind that's dangerous. Once it starts, you can't stop it.

"We learned it from you, Dad!" Dani said. "It was the second word Dana learned when she was a baby."

"Third," Dana corrected. "'Bite me,' were words one and two. Are you getting dementia, Dad?"

They were rolling. "You and Mom used to sit in separate rooms and send us back and forth, repeating horrible phrases," Dani said, barely able to get the words out between howls. "'Scrotum breath' comes to mind."

Dana chimed in. "And then, Dani said it to your boss that night you guys had him and his wife with the fake boobs over for dinner. Mom never forgot that one."

I still remembered my dismay. I wanted to be serious, but the contagion had infected me, too. "Your mother was way worse. Don't get me started on her potty mouth."

"Remember when she lost her temper at parents' night last fall?" Dani snorted, "And she told Genevieve's mom to, 'Kiss my high hairy one, you skank!'"

Dana's laugh was almost a shriek. "And you immediately asked Dad, 'what's a high hairy one, Daddy?'"

They had me. Tears rolled down my cheeks. "And I said, 'you're old enough to know one when you see one.'"

Dani could barely breathe. "Genevieve's mom stuck up her nose and said, 'See what happens to girls who come from a broken home?'"

Dana delivered the coup de grâce, a spot-on impression of Patty. "And Mom said, 'You should talk, you slut. You've had more semen than an admiral's wife.'"

Would Mallory even be interested in me after my kids shared these family secrets? I doubted it.

The mirth subsided. But my discomfort was just beginning.

"Can I ask you a question, Dad?" Dani's voice still had the jiggle of unspent laughter. "How did things go after Dana and I left you with Miss Mallory?"

I acted conspiratorially. "Can you girls keep a secret?"

Dana nodded, "Of course we can!"

"Well, so can I."

They both groaned. "Dad!" Dani whined. "That's a movie line from that chick flick Mom likes with Ted Danson in it."

Dana scrunched up into a pout. "Come on, Daddy. I told you all about Henry. Is Miss Mallory a good kisser?"

"Yeah," Dani chimed in. "How will we learn what to do with boys unless you tell us your war stories? That's what parents do."

I shook my head. "Any boy who is worth your time will protect your reputation and keep your secrets."

The two giggled with glee. "Oh. Dad got lucky Saturday night!"

"Okay, okay. I give up." I raised my hands in surrender. "It's been tough for me since your mom left. Yes, I get lonely and miss having a woman in my life. But I did something wrong the first time. I don't regret a thing because your mother gave me you two beautiful girls. I'm afraid to get serious with anybody, especially now with all this Corona uncertainty. I want a soulmate. I'm still hurting and need to figure out what my mistakes were so I won't make them again."

Dani rubbed my arm. "It takes two to tango, Dad. Mom's new husband is suffering just as much as you did. She's a hot mess and always has been. Hasn't your shrink told you that this is not your fault?"

I tried to remember if the doc had used those words.

"We love you, Daddy," Dana said, gripping my arm. "And we know you've done everything in your power to give us a wonderful start. Miss Mallory would be a lucky lady to have you in her life."

I held my daughters close. "You guys have always made me proud. I love you…"

"… to the moon and back," they said in unison as if I had just said the most boring thing ever. "We know."

"I only have one question," Dana said. "And you can be totally honest with us about it."

"I'll try, baby. What is it?"

"Does Miss Mallory scream during sex like Mom does?"

I put my girls in twin headlocks, rubbing the tops of their skulls with my fists.

"You two can be angels one minute and satanic sirens the next! Who's up for a Sunday swim?"

CHAPTER EIGHT

MALLORY
Working with Andrew over Zoom on Monday was uncomfortable. I couldn't take my eyes off of his image on the screen. And thank goodness for his ability to concentrate on the task at hand. I felt tongue-tied every time he asked me a question.

When I came home from work, I saw the envelope taped to my garage door. The card inside was one of those heart-melters with two little kids holding hands.

Mal,

I'm so glad that Ella is okay. She's a wonderful kid, and you are a terrific mom.

All joking aside, I'll never forget Friday. We were both in a vulnerable moment, so don't feel any strings attached to what happened. When we get past this work project, I would love to get to know you better, at your pace and in your time.

With admiration,

Andy

I wanted strings attached. That next night, alone in my bed, I conjured up memories of our encounter, swirling myself into orgasm, with the Greedy Girl Thrusting Rabbit vibrator that now bore Andrew's name, as I imagined replaying every scene over and over in my head.

But in the light of day, reality set in. We both brought baggage to the table. I didn't really know this man at all. And we both owed it to Ed to keep centered on our jobs. My unworthiness gene was screaming at me, "What value do you bring to a relationship? He deserves better."

I tried to put Andrew on the shelf; a one-night stand I'd never forget; a situation to aspire to… someday.

———

ANDREW

"How's your daughter?"

It took a moment to decipher the face behind the mask and the eyes that smiled at me in the frozen food aisle of the grocery store.

The doc from the emergency room looked out of place in street clothes and without the white lab coat and the stethoscope that hung around her neck, dancing in time with her chest as she walked.

"That was kind of you to attribute her blue eyes to me," I said. "But I'm just a neighbor, and her mom is a professional colleague. Thanks for helping us out."

The doc's eyebrows raised. I could see her sizing me up. "Pull down the mask for a second and let me make a memory of your face."

I did, conjuring up a dimpled smile for her. She was pleased by what she saw. "Very nice. What's with all the Lean Cuisines in your shopping cart?"

I shrugged. "Single dad. Joint custody of teenagers on the weekends. When they aren't around to make sure I eat properly, I revert to these things."

"There's enough sodium in those things to give you a stroke."

I pointed to the Oreos in my cart. "That's why I buy these. Doesn't sugar offset salt?"

The doc smirked. She knew I was playing with her. "You can do better than that. You should let me cook for you sometime."

I whipped up an expression of mock concern. Her statement spoke volumes. I needed confirmation. "What would your significant other say?"

She laughed, picked up a cucumber from her cart, and spoke to it. "Gerald? Meet my good friend…" The doc let the sentence hang in the air, expecting me to complete it.

"Andrew," I said with a slight bow, "I hope you don't think I'm trying to home in on your woman, Gerald. I hear that vegetables stick together, and I don't want the carrots and celery to attack me when I get home."

The doc flipped her cuke in a perfect three-sixty, catching it on the fly and returning it to its brothers in her cart. "No time for anything significant outside of work these days. And most men are intimidated by a woman who's smarter than they are."

The doc didn't intimidate me. And brains always turned me on. With Mal keeping her distance, I was still a free agent. "If you cook," I said, "I'll supply the wine and do the dishes."

She proffered a business card and scribbled an address and cell number on the back. "I work half-days on Wednesday. Six o'clock? Pino Grigio."

"Sounds great," I said. "But you barely know me."

Her smile was attractive, confident, hungry. "I'd like to know you…barely." She ran the tip of her tongue across a set of perfect white teeth.

I patted the cucumbers in her cart. "Sorry, guys. Please, don't be jealous."

Her jeans were tight enough to reveal the contours of a gym rat. The baggy sweater she wore did its best to minimize the visual impact of what I surmised was a beautiful balcony. I pulled my own biz card out of my wallet. She studied it, obviously pleased that my career aspirations put me into her orbit.

We pointed our carts toward the checkout. "I'm Jillian," she said. "You've only got a few items. You can go ahead of me."

I shook my head. "My dad always taught me that women come first."

Jillian shivered. "We're gonna get along just fine."

CHAPTER NINE

M ALLORY

My attorney called. "Time to re-budget," he said. "Elliot's company is struggling, and he got a temporary reprieve from the judge on alimony payments."

"Fuck, Ted! I'm just getting by with the income I have now. Does this guy remember he has a daughter with special needs?"

My lawyer tried to sound sympathetic. It wasn't working. "It's the pandemic, Mal. The thing is impacting everyone. You're lucky to have a job. Hopefully, things will pick up in six to twelve months and the cash can start flowing again."

Six to twelve months! Shit! I couldn't make it for six to twelve weeks, what with the therapists, doctors' appointments, and quarterly lab tests.

I thanked Ted for his concern and called Millie. I needed a shoulder to cry on.

I bribed Ella's sitter to stay late and met my best friend

at one of the carefully spaced outdoor tables set up by our favorite local bistro.

Millie was the free spirit I wished I could be. Our friendship went back to elementary school. We shared promiscuity, boyfriends, college, and divorce in common. But unlike me, Millie was kidless. Her job at the greeting card shop had evaporated with the onset of the pandemic, but she didn't seem to want for money.

"How do you do it?" I asked Millie that warm Wednesday evening. "You don't seem to have any means of financial support, but you're always buying clothes and jewelry and don't want for anything?"

"Is this stupid Covid thing starting to impact your bank account?" Millie wondered.

"Ted called. Elliot's business is crashing, and he got the judge to waive alimony for up to a year."

"You're the company's star employee," Millie said, sipping her chardonnay. "Ask your boss for a raise."

I shook my head. "Not politically correct in this environment. I feel lucky to be working at all. How in the hell do you do it, Millie?"

My friend's eyes scanned the area to see if anyone else was within earshot. She opened her Coach purse and tossed a card onto the table. The word "Donna" was centered on the card. A web address was printed beneath it.

———

ANDREW

Dr. Jillian Walcott lived in a home appropriate for a chief attending physician at a children's hospital. The back-yard bordered the 10th hole of one of the city's most exclusive golf courses. The bag full of Ping clubs by the sliding glass door told me she sometimes snuck in some stick time after work.

The brands that adorned her living room wine rack made me embarrassed to reveal the mid-grade Costco Pino Grigio that was my contribution. But Jillian wasn't one who wore her success on her sleeve.

She greeted me at the door in spandex pants that left little of her exquisite ass to the imagination. A white button-down blouse was covered by an apron with "I Live to Cook" embroidered on it. The black hair she kept bunned up at work cascaded over her shoulders. Reading glasses balanced on the end of a cute, perky nose.

"Come on in, soldier. Crack that bottle, and let's medicate while I burn our dinner."

Of course, she was joking about that second part. Jillian's culinary adventures were well documented in a half dozen award plaques she arranged in Feng Shui perfection on a free kitchen wall.

I snagged a corkscrew from her wine rack and poured us grown-up-sized grape juice portions.

"What's for supper?" I asked, watching the steam rise from half a dozen pots and pans on her hand-made French La Cornue range. I knew enough about the hardware to make the connection between the brand and Julia Child's artistry. "George Clooney and Brad Pitt would be pleased."

"Amateurs," Jillian groused. "A hundred grand for a stove and range is just a status symbol for those hunks. I wouldn't eat their food." She looked over the top of her reading glasses to make eye contact. "But I'd definitely let them eat me."

Suddenly uncomfortable, I handed her a glass. "To whatever it is you are creating," I said, trying to divert her attention from the body inspection she was clearly giving me.

"Spaghetti and meat balls," Jillian answered, clinking glasses, sucking a third of the wine down in a single gulp, and focusing on her work. "Every ingredient homemade, the second-best thing you'll consume tonight."

I assumed she meant the wine. Her eyes told me something else.

———

MALLORY

"Who is Donna?" I asked Millie, inspecting the sparse business card. "And how is she involved in your income stream? Don't tell me you've fallen for some multi-level sales thing."

"Donna is me," my friend said. She spread her arms to frame her body. "And this is my business."

I was totally confused. Millie didn't have anything near a model's figure. Was she teaching yoga on the side?

"You're gonna have to tell me more, Millie. I'm not getting it."

Millie looked around to see if anyone was within earshot. She leaned forward and whispered, "I'm an escort."

I still didn't get it, and she knew it. With more than a little exasperation, she said, "I get paid to fuck people."

I was stunned. "You are a prostitute?"

"The politically correct term is 'sex worker.' I have a long list of very satisfied clients who follow my rules and pay me handsomely for my…services."

"Geeze, Millie! Are you serious?"

"And I'll tell you something. After a few bumps at the beginning, I'm loving the work. I have more business than I can handle, and my clients are *very* appreciative. I'm coming up on two years and I have no plans to slow down."

I tried to picture my friend riding reverse cowgirl on some stranger's cock. It was hard not to laugh.

"Aren't you worried about STDs or some creepy guy hurting you?"

Millie's tired smile told me she'd heard that one before.

"We all get checked regularly. They have to bring proof that they are Covid negative. And my gynie and I are on a first-name basis."

"What does he think about this new job of yours?"

Millie studied the sun rays that painted red prisms on the tabletop through her wine glass. "Attitudes are changing, Mal. The oldest profession is getting a makeover. Girls are showing their twats on the internet and earning twenty grand a year. I earn that in a month."

"But it's still against the law," I said.

"I guess if the cops wanted to target me, they could. But in this city, it's 'live and let live.'" Millie shot me a cryptic look, "You would be surprised who some of my clients are. We definitely take care of one another."

"But why, Millie? Is this a way of getting back at your ex? It can't just be about the money."

"When I see pleasure in a man's eyes, I feel worthy, Mal. I've never liked this overstuffed body. But my customers do. Beyond the lifestyle it affords me, it's affirming."

The whole thing was giving me the creeps. "I don't know, Millie. I'm not sure it's that simple. Why are you telling me this?"

My friend took my hands in hers. "Because I think you'd be great at it, Mal. Look at your situation. You work from home, have flexible hours…" Millie stopped to drive her next point home. "And you're beautiful. You've got the skills. I remember many a college night when we could ride a dozen guys in an evening and leave each one begging for more. And having a kid only augmented God's gifts." Millie reached over and thumped my bra with an index finger. "You're so damn attractive that you'll be rolling in cash in no time."

Millie took a taste of her wine, a shiver running through her body. "The money is great, and the sex is fantastic. I come so many times a day that I leave Mr. Hitachi in the dresser at night." She gave me a sideways glance. "I wonder if you could sell all of those vibrators in a garage sale?"

I pulled back, crossing my arms as if protecting a pack of newborn kittens. "Give up my favorite authors? Never!"

Millie's expression turned serious. "Look, Mal. These are unusual times. We do what we have to, to provide for ourselves. I'm just telling you that if you're careful, your financial troubles will be over and you'll be having the best sex of your life, every day."

I couldn't get the image of Millie sucking off some overweight pervert out of my head. "Do any of them look like Fred Penoyer?"

Millie grimaced. "Fat Freddie? No! Like I said, you pick them. The demand far out-strips the supply. So you only have to strip for guys who turn you on."

Millie bit her lip and thought for a moment. "Ya know, I heard that Fat Freddie's lost a lot of weight and is a dot com millionaire." She picked up her phone from the table and started tapping text into it. "I think I'll see if I can find a recent picture."

"Be serious, Mil," I said. "What if I don't like a customer?"

"You choose the clients. They may raise their hands,

but you decide who gets to enter the golden chamber of ecstasy."

Andrew's face chose that moment to flash before me. "What I want is a stable, loving relationship, not a revolving door of dicks."

Millie closed her eyes, tilting her head back, a warm smile creasing her face. "I'll tell ya, Mal, I've never been happier, and with everyone on lockdown, the men have never been hornier. Let me show you the ropes. If you decide you don't like it, you can bail. But don't judge the entree until you've tasted the sauce."

The check came. Millie grabbed it. "How about a test drive? I have a way cool customer who is interested in a threesome."

CHAPTER TEN

ANDREW
Jillian's dinner surpassed my every expectation. She was clearly as gifted in the kitchen as she was at the hospital.

As we finished our meal, a woman appeared in the dining room. "Can I get you anything else, Dr. Walcott?" she said in a thick European accent.

Jillian shook her head. "We're good, Toni. You can head home. I'll do the dishes tonight."

"No need, ma'am. Already done. I'll be back tomorrow for the usual house cleaning. Are there any special instructions?"

Jillian thought for a moment. "We'll change the bed sheets. Aside from that, wash whatever is in the hamper and we can call it good."

Toni bowed and disappeared as magically as she had materialized. Jillian and I watched her butt sway back and forth as she left.

"Toni?" I said.

"Reliable and punctual four times a week. Hell if I'm

going to do housework with these hands." She rubbed her palms together, taking my measure. "These are reserved for other activities."

Jillian wasn't talking about surgery.

"The way you were looking at Toni, I began to wonder if you were grading her wardrobe or her ass."

Jillian winked. "I love men. But there are things women know how to do best. I don't discriminate in the bedroom."

No doubt. I was physically attracted to Jillian. In her tax bracket, I had no idea how much of the body was nature's creation but what was poured into that shirt and spandex was beyond alluring. And Mallory was still on my mind. Was it simply the fact that she broke a long sexual dry spell? Or was there something more to the attraction?

Jillian must have been thinking the same thing. She leaned back in the leather dining room chair and undid the top button of her shirt, revealing some magnificent cleavage.

"So tell me about the mom. Are you guys a thing, or are you just a good neighbor?"

I tried to sound casual. "Like I said, we're colleagues. Her boss is a college buddy, and his firm is a client."

Another button undone. The breasts were at least double Ds, maybe larger. "Are you romping through Cupid's grove with her, or are you 'just friends?'"

"I don't know that you could even call us friends. Professional colleagues is more like it. I was in the right place at the right time to help when her daughter got that spider bite."

"Was sex part of what lead to your divorce?"

Her directness stunned me. "You ask the questions, don't you?"

"We're grown-ups, Andrew. You're what I would call

the perfect package. Successful in business, the kind of guy who drops everything to save a damsel in distress, and…" She licked her teeth with that tongue again. "You're making me wet. I just want to know whether or not to ply you with Viagra before I fuck you."

I raised an eyebrow. "Are all female doctors like this?"

She flipped the third button free of its clasp. Two gloriously erect nipples popped into view.

"Want to find out?"

———

MALLORY

"I can't believe you talked me into this, Millie."

Dinner with my best friend had a catch. She had a client tonight who was interested in a threesome. Millie's goal had been to convince me to be that third person.

With visions of overdrafts dancing in my head, I had said, "Yes."

"It's gonna be great, Mal. You'll love Roger. Super nice. Super rich and hung like a Clydesdale."

I was no prude. While I could sell the conservative act in the real world, I was as hungry as the next girl for washboard abs, bulging biceps, and a nice thick cock.

But my paradigms about sex work were all negative. I was having second thoughts about Millie's threesome idea… until the doorbell rang.

The man who Millie greeted was gorgeous! He could have walked right off of the cover of *GQ*. Six feet two inches tall, definitely with a body sculpted by an expensive trainer, a solid gold Rolex watch graced his left wrist. No wedding ring.

I could see over Millie's shoulder as she checked her cell

phone. Her bank app blinked as one thousand dollars was added to her balance.

Roger's smile was warm, not at all the creep I expected. He held out a hand. "I'm Roger. You're everything Millie said and more, Gina."

So now I'm "Gina"?

I took his hand. The grasp was firm but tender.

"It's a pleasure to meet you, Roger," I heard myself say in an alluring voice that was nothing like the executive I also pretended to be.

Mille giggled, taking Roger's other hand. "It's her first time, so we'll be teaching her."

My friend pulled us toward the huge new bathroom and master bedroom combination she had recently added to her home. "You're gonna love the shower."

———

ANDREW

Jillian was definitely an aggressor. She had me naked and spread eagle on her bed in minutes, standing at the foot, continuing her strip tease.

"I like to watch men get erect," she said, releasing the last of the buttons and sliding the shirt off of her shoulders. "The tits aren't real." She cupped her breasts and held them up for my inspection. "They're better than real. What do you think?"

Her nipples stuck out like a pair of red safety cones. I could see the wetness marking her spandex.

"Magnificent. Was it cash or trade?"

Jillian laughed. "This is gonna be fun. I like your attitude. I paid for them." She slid her thumbs to highlight two tiny dots where the flesh met her chest. "Expandable," she said. "I've got the saline injectors right here in the bedroom if you want them even bigger."

"Jesus, Jillian," was the best I could muster.

"I let a little of the air out for work. Tits can get in the way when you work in tight spots. Do you like them bigger?"

Hers hung with near perfection, like a sixteen-year-old who won the puberty prize. Jillian bent over and moved her shoulders so the substantial orbs swung from side to side.

"I can lactate if I want. Never had kids but wanted to see if there was any science behind this whole 'adult nursing relationship' thing."

The conversation was having the doctor's desired effect. My cock was rising like a rocket launcher.

"You are a fucking pervert, Jillian," I said. "How do you stay licensed with that licentious mind?"

Jillian was clearly pleased. "Licentious! I bet you're a demon at Scrabble, too. How do you like your pussies? Hairy or shaved?"

With that, she peeled off the spandex to reveal a practically perfect ass and one of the most beautiful Brazilians I had ever seen. Jillian parted her pussy lips with a pair of fingers, sliding them upward to reveal a pink, pulsing clit.

"The rest is all natural," she said as my cock began to throb in anticipation. "Is your oral sex as good as your sense of humor?"

"Mightier than the sword," I said, revealing a tongue that had long ago perfected how to touch the tip of my nose.

Jillian caught her breath. "Well! This is going to be fun." She tilted her head. "How do you feel about handcuffs?"

———

MALLORY

Millie had told me that hygiene is the first thing the pros tend to. That included both parties showering and comparing their health paperwork. They made an exception for me with the latter, but I was fully included in the preparations.

Millie and I washed our client from head to toe in the biggest shower stall I had ever seen. Multiple shower heads rained down upon us as we prepared Roger for the festivities.

Millie gave me a "follow my lead" look and knelt down to massage Roger's massive cock. She wasn't kidding. This guy was stud farm material. I instantly thought of the Clydesdales in beer commercials they show during the football championship. My friend grinned and made a chomping motion with her jaws, motioning me to join her.

"You take his balls. I'll do the rest."

With that, "Donna" circled the head of Roger's dick with her mouth, grasping his shaft with both hands as she began to suck.

College memories came rushing back. We had been sorority sisters and knew a thing or two about the craft. I gently massaged Roger's balls with my fingers, kneeling so that I could take each into my own mouth and tickle his scrotum with my tongue.

Roger's moans were a huge turn-on. He leaned back against the tile, pressing his hips forward so we could see his enormous erection in all its glory.

Millie attacked with abandon, deep-throating the whole thing again and again like a side-show sword swallower.

"You've been holding out on me," I said. "Learning new skills on the side, eh?"

"On the side, on top, on the bottom, standing on my head," she said, the head of Roger's cock pressed deeply into her cheek. "I'll teach you everything."

I stood and put Roger's hand on one of my breasts while still massaging his balls. I could feel the twitch that I knew preceded climax.

Millie knew her client well. His grunt was the sign. Roger's hips started to undulate, and his ejaculation began.

"Look at this," Millie giggled.

She guided his squirting shaft, so her own two tits were soon covered with his semen. I could see Roger's eyes widen at the sight.

"Well done, Roger! Well done! You're better than a power-washer."

When he began to subside, Millie wiped a swath of his production into a palm and held it between the two of us.

"Have a taste," she beckoned.

What the hell? Why not? We both licked his juices together, making the same satisfying noises that instantly made our college fucks hard again as our client watched in awe.

"I told you Gina was really good," Millie said, swallowing the last of his production. "Now for the main act!"

CHAPTER ELEVEN

ANDREW

Jillian was definitely a dominatrix. Perhaps having to be so compassionate at work caused the need to express her other side in the bedroom. Or maybe my first assessment that I had a nymphomaniac by the tale was the better conclusion.

Patty and I had experimented with a Dom during our marriage, and I wasn't at all claustrophobic. The handcuffs actually felt pretty good locked to the custom-built headboard. They gave me additional leverage for the gymnastics.

Once Jillian had put the keys on her nightstand, she began her work. She licked every inch of my erect cock, squeezing my balls right to the point of pain. She kept eye contact to watch my reaction, smiling when she saw my startled appreciation.

Then she crawled toward the headboard, snaking her legs behind my arms and grabbing the top of the headboard as she lowered her wet cunt toward my mouth.

"Show me what you've got, cowboy," she challenged. "Make me come with that glorious tongue."

I was impressed with the tone and strength of the muscles in Jillian's legs. She hovered just above me until I could smell the juices that were dampening her perfectly groomed pussy.

"I gotta warn you, though," she added. "I'm a squirter."

I was up to the challenge. I began by kissing the area, then tickling her labia with my tongue before parting her lips and sliding it deep into her cunt. The sound of Jillian's guttural moans told me I was right on the money, and I could feel her clit pulsing against my upper lip.

"OMG," Jillian moaned. "I feel like I'm getting the most incredible vaginal exam of my life."

I rolled her delectable juices around in my mouth. "My professional assessment is that everything is in order. However, I recommend aggressive palpation of the clitoral region."

"He talks like a gynecologist, and tongue fucks me like a snake." Jillian tilted her head toward the ceiling. "Thank you, God!"

I pulled her throbbing pearl into my mouth and tickled it with my swirling tongue. I alternated this with long, languid labia licks.

I slipped my pink sword inside of her and began tongue fucking Jillian with abandon. I could see the muscles in her legs tighten. Her ass began to roll back and forth, in sync with my oral thrusts.

Jillian's breaths became short puffs, increasing in speed until she involuntarily inhaled, emitting a guttural burst that I would come to associate with her climax.

And yes, the doctor was a squirter. I felt a gush of warm juices roll down my chin and onto my neck as she came.

Jillian dis-entwined her legs from my shoulders and fell on top of me, kissing my mouth and licking her juices off of my chin and neck.

"Balls on buttered toast," she whispered. "That's a first. I didn't think a tongue fucking could make me explode like that."

I wondered how many other men before me had heard those same words. "You've had practice."

"Lots," she panted. "Want to see what I learned?"

I gave Jillian a licentious look. "Release my wrists and I'll give you a second course first."

My partner continued her licking.

"It's important to keep the operating theater sterile. And I kinda have a thing for tasting the liquid products of the sex act."

"Like fine wine without the grapes?" I asked.

Jillian wrapped a set of fingers around my sack. "Just wait till I start tickling your grapes."

"Get rid of the cuffs," I commanded. "And I'll show you how many ways I can make you come."

Jillian shivered in anticipation. I've never seen someone move faster with a set of keys. It reminded me of my kids when it was their turn with the car.

I grabbed her ass and threw her backward onto the mattress, pressing her legs high into the air as I continued to eat her out.

"Now I'm in control," I growled, pushing her shoulders against the bed and turning my attention to her erect nipples.

Whatever the surgeons had done during her augmentation didn't dim the sensitivity of Jillian's nerve endings. She writhed beneath me as I lightly bit her areolae, guiding my cock toward the warmth that awaited me.

Now that I knew how Jillian operated, I didn't linger at

the doctor's opening like my other lovers preferred. Instead, I slammed my cock deep inside, grasping her arms for balance.

I still don't know where my energy came from, but as Jillian begged for more, I increased the pace and intensity of our intercourse, pummeling her pussy until she draped her head over the edge of the bed and squealed as she climaxed for the second time.

The volume alone would have shocked an ordinary man, but I had been married to a screamer for seventeen years. I knew this was a sign of success. "I think I just heard glasses breaking in the kitchen," I said.

"Keep it up and I'll sing you an aria," Jillian said, grabbing my face and looking into my eyes with undiminished hunger.

I wasn't finished with her yet. Wrapping my arms around Jillian's waist, I pulled her upward as I lay on my back.

She watched in amazement as I lowered her onto my still rock-hard cock and grasped the cheeks of her ass, sliding her cunt back and forth over my pubic mound as I fucked her.

Jillian fell forward, found my mouth, kissed me passionately, and took control of the proceedings again. Her grind quickened, and the friction began to do its work.

It was my turn to groan. I let go and filled her slit with jet after jet of my own warm white spurts.

Jillian's smile telegraphed satisfaction, victory. "Woo hoo! That buttered my bread, big boy."

Perhaps, at last, I had satiated her.

"Where did this explosive lust come from," I asked, still dizzy from the extraordinary experience.

Jillian sighed. "Both of my parents were doctors. Their

patients came first. I was that only child who never got any attention. The only affirmation they ever gave me was when I followed them into the profession."

"Why pediatrics?"

"It's a kid substitute. I could never subject a biological child to my absent lifestyle. I get my fix at the office."

"So, this is how you affirm your spiritual existence?"

"It's my drug. Some docs abuse narcotics. Some drink. I can last a week on a good fuck." She tilted her head, flicking her eyebrows. "And you are one good fuck. I want you every Wednesday night from now on, Andrew."

"Why do I suddenly feel objectified?" I joked.

"Just the object of my affection," she shot back, giving my softening cock a squeeze. "I admit to having what some might call an 'unhealthy obsession' with fucking. My therapist will be pleased that I've found a productive way to keep it under control."

"I'll send you a bill," I said. "And I don't take insurance."

Jillian wrapped an arm around me and kissed me tenderly on the cheek.

"You're well worth the investment. What can I do for you in return?"

An idea came to me. "I know a little girl who deserves the best pediatrician in town. Got room for another patient?"

She bit my earlobe. "Got time for another round?"

CHAPTER TWELVE

MALLORY
It had been years since my last threesome. But as the saying goes, it's like riding a bicycle. Millie and I quickly found our rhythm, taking turns riding Roger and pressing our tits into his mouth.

Millie had alerted me that this was our client's fetish. I found myself totally enjoying pressing my nipples against the suction of his lips.

My girlfriend bounced up and down like Roger was an exercise ball. I was so focused on my work that I was surprised to hear her moan with glee as she came.

The sound energized Roger. He began to stroke his massive dick as Millie moved up to his face to relive me. My girlfriend kissed Roger deeply while rubbing her tits against his chest.

I realized it was my turn on the merry-go-round and playfully slapped Roger's hand away from his cock, so I could slide it inside of me.

He was so big that it hurt at first, but my pussy quickly

adjusted, and I began my grind, clinching his cock with every cycle.

Apparently, this was something he had not experienced with Mille. His moans grew louder, even as my girlfriend switched from deep, erotic kisses to pressing her own massive breasts into his mouth.

I began to understand how someone could be attracted to a more substantial body and admired Millie's confidence and the care with which she attended to her client's needs.

I was suddenly motivated to make Roger come, rolling my knees back and forth to deepen and hasten my grind.

I heard Millie whisper into Roger's ear as she shoved a breast deeper into his mouth.

"Now, baby. Show Gina what you've got. Show her now, baby."

The words must have set Roger off. He suddenly opened his mouth, gasping and grabbing my hips with two strong hands.

Roger pressed upward, his full measure tickling the edge of my cervix, and came.

The eruptions felt like a pressure washer. Millie stroked Roger's hair. "That's it, baby. That's it. Give it all to Gina. Give her every last drop."

With a final thrust, Roger collapsed, panting and satiated as his two hookers snuggled into the warmth of his strong arms.

———

ANDREW

Jillian fucked me in her bedroom. She fucked me in her living room. We fucked on the kitchen counter. And she took me one more time as I was about to get in the shower.

I didn't think I had it in me, but I was pleased that I could keep up with someone who was clearly a nymphomaniac.

"See you next Wednesday? Same time, same cock?" Jillian said, wrapping her arms around my waist as I edged toward the front door and freedom. "You're one of the best I've ever had."

"*One* of the best?" I asked in mock displeasure. "I want to know who was better so I can show you what you were missing."

I regretted that bravado almost as soon as I said it. Jillian was a tigress in the bedroom, but I didn't like her doctor's ego and what felt like an empty emotional bank account.

I wanted Mallory.

Jillian held her embrace, turning us around so her back was blocking the door.

"It's still early. How about one more for the road?"

———

MALLORY

Millie kept a strict eye on the clock. I wasn't sure how much time Roger had bought, but when it was over, she switched off the passion and reverted to her usual friendly but reserved self.

We took separate showers and dressed.

Roger held my hand in his as he was about to leave. The gratitude in his eyes touched me. "Thank you, Gina. This was a first for me, an evening I'll always remember. And you helped make it so."

As he let go, I saw ten crisp one-hundred-dollar bills in my palm.

Millie grinned. "Next week, Roger? Same time, same place?"

Roger bowed. "I will look forward to it, Donna. You always over-deliver."

———

"SEE HOW EASY THAT WAS?" MILLIE SAID, CRACKING open a bottle of Merlot. "A toast to your first customer. Donna and Gina! What a team!"

"Now wait a minute, Millie," I said, holding up a hand. "This was a one-time-only thing. I have a career that would crater if anybody found out ."

Millie upended her glass. How she could be so energetic after all of that cardio was a thing to behold. "Relax, girlfriend. Nobody is going to find out. These guys are just as interested in keeping things on the down-low as you are."

"And where did you learn to deep throat a guy? I don't remember you doing that in school."

"Everything's on the internet, Mal. I can teach you how to swallow a sword and enjoy every inch."

I shook my head. "You're a fucking pervert, Millie. You always have been."

My best friend grinned. "And it's built an addition onto my house, paid for two trips to Europe, and that brand new SUV in my garage." She paused, still smiling but giving me one of those reality check looks I never liked seeing. "Tell the truth. Did you enjoy our little encounter with Roger?"

I had to admit that I had. With Millie there, I felt safe. The thought of being in control was something I never knew with Elliot. And the sex was downright awesome.

"Build your portfolio carefully, and that can be you,

Mal. I've got a money guy who is socking my earnings away. Another two years and I'll never have to work again."

My own head was spinning. Without time to even think about what I had done, I had sold my body to a stranger. And I had totally enjoyed the experience.

"Give it some consideration, Mal," Millie said as she swatted my ass at the front door. "I'll be right beside you, so you can learn from my mistakes. I promise you won't regret it."

Mistakes? What mistakes?

As I limped to my car with one thousand dollars in my purse and a sore pussy between my legs, I thought about the financial security I could provide for Ella. I thought about the personal power I had regained in the bedroom. There were dangers, too, many of which I knew nothing about. Uncertainty bounced around my brain like a pinball.

In the midst of the confusion, I knew one thing for sure.

I wanted Andrew.

CHAPTER THIRTEEN

ANDREW

As the months passed, I discovered there are good things about having a doctor as a fuck buddy...beyond the sex. Jillian was serious about adding value in return. She got me into the vaccine trial, so I got one of the first Covid shots. And Ella became her one and only personal patient.

The beautiful little girl was Mal's baby, but I think Jillian could sense there was a psychic connection between Ella's mom and me. Jillian was grateful that I had someone who could fill her emotional void.

She and Mallory became fast friends. Mal and I were still all business, and Jillian respected that. She never revealed our secret.

"I'm getting to know the doctor who helped us when Ella had that spider bite," Mal told me one day at the end of a long video conference call.

I tried not to sound too interested. "Tell me more."

"She's really very nice, incredibly skilled, and treats Ella like a princess. She called me out of the blue a couple of months ago to ask if Ella had a primary care pediatrician and offered her services. Can you imagine Ella being cared for by a chief attending physician? And I've never received a bill."

I knew Jillian and I would have a conversation about that on Wednesday night. "Your girl deserves the best," was all I said.

———

"So, how long has this Mal thing been going on?" I asked after the maid had been dismissed and Jillian and I were stripping for each other in her bedroom. "Have you told her about us?"

"That's your story to tell," she said.

I was still nervous about telling it.

My doctor fuck buddy wanted an intellectual equal who wasn't afraid of a dominating, smart woman. And, of course, she wanted my body.

My Wednesday nights had become a procession of sumptuous, home-cooked meals, deep conversations about the complexities and challenges of pediatric medicine, and the wildest sex of my life.

I saw Mal almost every day, too, virtually. The furlough plan we had crafted for Ed was as well received as could be expected. He was lauded in the press as a "compassionate, caring boss" and was able to maintain profit margins that kept investors happy and customers satisfied.

I wanted to come clean with Mal about Jillian but couldn't bring myself to do it.

Why? Mallory was a one-night stand, a confidence builder that reminded me I was still attractive to women. And keeping our distance was appropriate since we were essentially professional colleagues. At least that's how I rationalized it.

My girls totally saw through the charade.

"You should end this libido fest with that doctor," Dani said one Saturday evening. "I like Mallory better."

"Yeah," my youngest chimed in. "She's normal. Dr. Dick-Me is an out-and-out nympho."

"Dr. Dick-Me?" I hadn't heard that one before.

"That's what we call her," Dana continued. "You're her 'vibrator with legs,' an inflatable man-toy who listens to her rambles and then goes away."

"She's getting everything she wants and then some," Dani added. "What are you getting?"

Dana redirected. "What do you want, Daddy?"

Six months later and I still wanted Mallory.

So I decided to call her.

———

MALLORY

With Millie, or "Donna, the Hooker," as my virtual manager, I was quickly in demand in the rarefied escort world.

That sounds like a euphemism, but it turned out to be a big part of the game. Many of my clients just wanted companionship, someone to take to dinner who looked good on their arm and listened to their tales of woe at work and at home.

I was a bit worried that we might run into Andrew, but in a world of six-foot separation and public masking, that never happened, thank god.

Some of my customers were unhappily married, others were single. As long as they adhered to Millie's strict rules of engagement, "Gina" was just fine with fulfilling their needs.

I felt my own self-confidence growing with my bank account. Elliot was a fading memory. Even my most self-absorbed clients cared more about me than my ex did. My HR skills made me a good listener. My reputation above the radar was growing. I began to receive calls and emails from underlings asking for advice. And my explorations in erotic ecstasy were off the charts.

Ella was getting the best medical and therapeutic attention possible. And I grew to love helping men feel good about themselves, learning the kinks that their significant others thought were silly or too wild.

I had my boundaries. Nothing up the ass. Condoms required for pussy sex. And mutually assured hygiene and health safety.

I was still not comfortable with having anyone come to my place. That was fine with Millie. She gave me access to her original master suite whenever I needed it. Some days, my clients were turned on by hearing her joyful screams as she rode her own customer at one end of the house while I was sucking off mine at the other end.

And I learned something else.

Roger must have spread the word about how one plus two was better than one plus one. More of Millie's customers wanted me to participate in the proceedings.

It was only a matter of time until we were confronted by a customer who wanted to watch two women make love.

I would soon discover that my definition of sexuality was about to change.

CHAPTER FOURTEEN

ANDREW

"Hey, buddy! I need a date."

Eddie always got to the point.

"I know we're in pandemic hell, but I've got two angel investors I know flying in on Friday. I've reserved a private room at the Maracaibo Grille, and I need some wing-people."

I was skeptical. "I don't know, Ed. We're all practicing distancing and masking. Outsiders spread this stuff."

"It's gonna be okay, Andy. These guys have money in big pharma and were first in line for the vaccine trial. They are walking anti-body factories. I know you and I are both pristine. I paid for our tests last week, and I'll pay for another one on Wednesday. The key question is, do you know a couple of women who have a similar obsession with staying germ-free who could escort us."

"Us?"

"Yeah, these guys are bringing their wives. I need females for them to talk to."

I still didn't like the setup. "So you ask a divorced guy with no life who never leaves his house to fix you up?"

"Hey, I've got an idea." Ed always had an idea. "I'll ask Mallory Michaels to be your date. You guys are working together on the furlough project. She's super smart and can make conversation. Tell her to bring a friend."

"She's your employee, Eddie. *You* ask her to bring a friend. I'll just show up."

Ed shut me down. "Won't work. I'll be coming off of an all-day zoom with the bankers. I'll need you and Mal to pick me up. Say six-thirty? The reservation's at seven."

The guy was the same deal maker I had known since we were in college. You couldn't say no. But I wasn't afraid to. "Naw, buddy. Leave me out of this one. I've got teenagers, and I'd never forgive myself if I brought Covid home."

It was as if my friend hadn't heard me. "Tell you what. A thousand bucks a piece as a performance bonus for all three of you. This is important, Andy. Six-thirty, Friday. Bring the Escalade. These guys will be impressed by the American iron. And make sure my date's gorgeous with a good sense of humor."

"Eddie," I was pleading. But my friend was already moving on.

"Gotta go, Andy. I'm late for another call. See you Friday. And tell Mal 'thanks' for me."

———

MALLORY

Andrew sounded sheepish when he called about Ed's thing with the rich people.

"I feel weird asking you to risk your life when it's your boss who should do the asking," he said. "Would you be willing to get a Covid test on Wednesday so we'd have results by Friday?"

"Our first date," I gushed. I wanted to lower the poor guy's anxiety level. "We're doing everything backward. Fuck first and see if we have stuff in common second. Is this how you always treat your women?"

"This isn't fair to you, Mal. The last thing I want to do is possibly expose you to Covid when you've got a baby at home."

I didn't yet want to tell him I was having almost weekly tests for everything from Corona to the clap.

"It will be okay, Andrew. And I'd love to eat at the Maracaibo on someone else's credit card. Let's do it."

There was silence on the other end of the line. "There's more. Ed wants us to get him a date. Apparently, these guys have wives, and he's determined to impress them all."

I knew exactly who I would ask. "I'll handle it, Andrew. My friend, Millie, will look great on his arm, and we'll charm the panties off of the spouses while you guys talk shop."

I could hear the relief in Andrew's voice. "You're a peach, Mallory. Ed says there's a grand in this for each of us, just in case we need money for a funeral."

"That's not funny," I said, even though my giggles gave away the fact that I thought it was. "Do I get your hot bod after? I guess I should have made that part of the deal before I said yes."

"The girls are doing a zoom party Friday night, and I feel like I should lurk around to eavesdrop. Can I make it up to you later?"

"I can think of a dozen ways you can make it up to me. And they all involve nudity."

Andrew was trying to maintain professional decorum.

It was so cute! "Mal, don't forget that we're still colleagues. Business before pleasure."

I sniffed. "You've gotta learn to break a few rules, my friend. If you caught Covid and died and never had me again, you'd regret it."

"If I died, I probably wouldn't have an opinion."

I could still feel the tension and was determined to break it. "If you die on me, I'll chase you to the gates of heaven and arm wrestle St. Peter to drag you back into my life."

That won the day. Andrew laughed. "You might have to do more than that, Mal. I think things might get a bit warm in the front office as they tally the books. Do you think you can convince Millie to join us on Friday?"

"Consider it done. I hope she doesn't torpedo both of our careers."

"Eddie gets what he gets. I told him this was a bad idea. See ya Friday."

CHAPTER FIFTEEN

ANDREW
I gobbled a Xanax and a shot of vodka before picking up the women on Friday night. The tests came back clean, and Ed promised me that his guests would maintain social distance.

The former was science. The latter was the unknown.

The Maracaibo Grille lived up to its reputation. The tuxedo penguins wore branded jet-black masks. They guided us to a private room complete with a private bar and two shapely servers. Their eyes could knock a guy out, and I'm sure Eddie wondered if the rest of their faces were just as alluring.

The masks we wore into the restaurant went into pockets and purses, and we got a good look at the enemy.

"Curt Whitman and Thomas Mardall, meet Andrew and Mallory, my human resource geniuses, and this," Eddie bowed toward Mal's best friend, "is Millie, my significant other."

Millie and Mal exchanged smirks. I could tell that

Millie was going to make the most of Ed's act. I was terrified.

Whitman grinned. "I pity you, Millie. Do you ever see the guy in person? He's the busiest CEO I've ever met."

Millie pinched Ed's ass. "Not nearly often enough, Curt. But I'm on the run a lot, too. I handle Ed's philanthropic interests."

I had no idea where this was headed, but it couldn't be anywhere good. I stuck out a hand to Whitman's escort. "We're horrible hosts. I'm Andrew."

"Adrian Bates. Curt's wife." she turned to Millie. "We definitely have to visit. I run the Whitman Foundation in San Francisco."

I shook Curt's hand. Mal exchanged executive grips with Thomas Mardall. "Call me Mal. Do you prefer Thomas or Tom?"

Mardall seemed warm and genuine. "Tom, please. I get so tired of people throwing Thomas around. It makes it sound like I'm a classy guy, instead of a lucky schmuck who bet on the right social network."

Mardall's lady punched his shoulder. "Tom's flaw is humility. The idiot founder wouldn't be a zillionaire without him." She took Mal's hand. "Roxie Mardall. How in holy hell did you furlough six-hundred people without a riot?"

Mal leaned close as if she were sharing the nuclear codes. "We bonused them for the weeks they had to wait for unemployment and are still paying health insurance." Mal brushed a finger across my cheek. "It was this guy's idea."

Millie signaled one of the masked beauties, eyeing her name tag and, no doubt, calculating the size of her bust. "Guys, this is Veronica. She's one of the two top team members here at the Maracaibo, and it's her job to make sure we are well-medicated before dinner. What can she get you to drink?"

The girl was behaving. In fact, she was playing the role of Ed's girlfriend like an Academy Award winner.

Millie wrapped an arm around Ed's waist, flashing him her bedroom eyes. "Honey, what's your pleasure tonight? Are we drinking wine or having a cocktail?"

"The usual, hon," Ed answered. "An old fashioned, please."

Millie smiled at Veronica. "Two old fashioned for us, please, Roni. But with brandy. Lecompte Secret Calvados, if you've got it."

Holy shit, I thought. That was three thousand dollars a bottle.

Whitman was impressed. "Make that three, please, Veronica."

"I'm in," Adrian added. "I remember when the best we could afford was Boone's Farm."

Mal and I ordered dirty martinis. I forget what the Mardalls ordered because Adrian Bates was taking Millie by the arm. "These guys will talk about making money all night. Let's go plot how we will spend it."

I turned to go after them, but Mal took my arm and held tight. "Enjoy the moment," she whispered. "Ed asked for this."

My date turned to Roxie Mardall. "So, tell me how you and Tom first met?"

When Mal was certain that I was staying put, she let me go, and I drifted into conversation with Ed and his investors.

Two rounds of drinks later, the servers invited us to sit. Menus were studied. Selections were made. And we settled into what I hoped would be small talk.

Boy, was I wrong.

Adrian Bates tossed the first-hand grenade. "So Ed, Millie tells me that your foundation is advocating the legalization of sex work and cannabis. She said it's a passion of yours."

How Ed held it together is still a mystery. I saw his eyes dart to mine. But he didn't miss a beat.

"Ya know, Adrian, on the surface, that sounds like something some stranger I just met tonight might say to embarrass me. But when you believe in something, you feel the fear and do it anyway."

"It just seems so odd when things like ignorance, poverty, and homelessness are still such huge, huge issues."

Ed sailed forward. "The disaffected often turn to prostitution as a last income resort. When well regulated, like it is in Nevada, it can be mutually beneficial. And if you get a couple of cocktails into any doctor, they will tell you that THC is truly a miracle drug, much less dangerous in recreational use than what we've been drinking tonight."

Adrian looked at Curt. "This is one amazing man, Curtis. Not afraid to take on controversy."

"The hallmark of a true entrepreneur," Curt said, raising his glass.

By now, my blood pressure was through the roof. I would have given up my credit cards and my keys for a joint at that moment.

"I'm fascinated," Roxie said, focusing on Millie. "Do you interact directly with sex workers?"

"Eddie insisted on it," Millie said, curling against my best friend's shoulder. "There are a number of women who treat it as a true profession and earn quite a good living. You've probably met someone recently who is in the business."

"I'd love to hear about The Whitman Foundation's focus," I said, trying to derail this freight train to disaster.

"Boring," Adrian answered. "We do what everyone else does. Right now, it's all pandemic stuff. Getting the disaffected into the vaccine trials, distributing masks, teaching kids about social distancing. When this craziness is over, we'll be back to funding symphonies and helping Bill and Melinda distribute condoms in Africa."

Adrian processed that last item. "I guess you could call that sex work."

"Ya know, honey," Millie said, gazing admiringly into Ed's eyes. "We ought to talk with Bill and Melinda about that. They need a catchy slogan like, 'A Rubber in Every Wallet.' She turned to Adrian. "What do you think, Adrian?"

I began to wonder if there was a god. Adrian was considering her answer when the servers appeared with our entrees.

Conversation shifted to how kids on Reddit could influence the stock market and Warren Buffett's investments in the development of supersonic executive jets.

"I am going to kill your best friend," I muttered to Mallory.

Mal put her hand over her mouth to stifle a grin. "I think the evening is going swimmingly. A master class in human resource psychology."

"A master class in how to start a dumpster fire," I whispered back. "God, let this thing be over."

Whoever was up there wasn't listening. Roxi Mardell leaned back in her chair and focused on Millie. "So, Millie, what does the data say is the most popular? Blow jobs, BDSM, or anal?"

CHAPTER SIXTEEN

A NDREW

After the Whitmans and the Mardalls were safely in their limo headed back to the airport, Ed cornered me outside the Maracaibo. "Do you two mind if I take Millie home? I had my assistant bring the McLaren, and I'd love to show her how fast that thing can go."

"I am *so* sorry," I said. "Millie can be a handful, but she's truly a sweet girl when you get to know her."

"She was terrific! Curt and Tom loved her. And the wives? They won't forget this visit for a long time."

My college buddy punched my chest and pulled his mask over his mouth. "Great job, Andy. Tell Mal that I'm doubling everyone's bonuses."

Millie and Mallory emerged from the ladies' room, giggling and chattering like my teenagers.

Ed held out his hand. "Millie, how would you like to see something I'm super proud of?"

Mal's friend pulled Ed to her and planted a prostitu-tional kiss on his lips. "There's nothing I would like more."

———

A very impressed valet brought Ed's half-million-dollar McLaren from the parking lot. My best friend held the passenger door for Millie. "I know a place where we can put this baby through her paces without a cop in sight."

Millie turned to wink at Mal and me. She grabbed Ed's crotch. "And I know a place where I can put this baby through his paces without a cop in sight."

The sports car peeled out, leaving a trail of rubber on the asphalt in front of the restaurant. With Mallory safely next to me in my SUV, I finally felt I could exhale.

"That was the most terrifying night of my life."

Mal broke into a fit of laughter. "What did Ed expect? He who makes last-minute demands deserves what he gets."

I was still incredulous. "But it didn't even phase him. The guy seemed to enjoy the whole horrific thing."

Mal leaned over and kissed me on the cheek. "We may have started something tonight that will change both Ed and Millie's lives."

The insanity of the entire experience suddenly felt totally hilarious. I mimicked Roxie's question. "So, Millie, what does the data say is the most popular? Blow jobs, BDSM, or anal?"

Mal exploded in mirth. "Millie didn't miss a beat. 'Correct me if I'm wrong, Eddie, but cock sucking out distances every other kink by a five to one.'"

Now, I was laughing, too. "And then, Adrian, of all people, asks, 'I thought masturbation was number one.'"

Mal delivered a spot-on Eddie impression. "And our boss shoots back, 'Jerking off is an individual sport. It's so universal that not even our foundation can keep track of the numbers."

"Ed doesn't have a foundation," I said, tears rolling down my cheeks. "He better hope they don't do a Google search for it on the airplane."

Mallory rolled her eyes. "Something tells me I'll be doing some 501(c)3 paperwork on Monday."

I put the vehicle in gear and felt a soft hand on my thigh. "Ella's spending the night with Amber. Want to go back to your place and eavesdrop on the girls?"

My world was spinning out of control. But at that moment, I couldn't have cared less.

CHAPTER SEVENTEEN

ANDREW
My cell rang at seven-thirty the next morning. I recognized the caller ID and answered with a feeling of impending doom.

"Morning, Ed. Are you calling for bail money?"

"Holy shit, Andy. Are all of Mallory's friends like Millie?"

That didn't tell me anything. I felt like I was walking through a minefield. "Millie is definitely not normal."

"Damn straight, she isn't. I'm just leaving her place. I missed a 6 am call with London."

I could hear the road noise over the hands-free system in Ed's car. "Want to talk about it, or are you calling to tell me that our twenty-year friendship is over?"

I recognized the beep that meant Ed was getting another call. "Awe shit. The lawyers."

"Do you need to take that?"

"Let 'em wait. I have to tell somebody about the last eight hours, or my head will explode. You're the only one I trust."

That was a first. Ed putting off business. This must be a doozy.

"So, I take Millie to this stretch of road that I know where we can wind the car up to two hundred miles per hour. 'This is the fastest production automobile made,' I tell her. 'I'm about to show you how fast.'

"'If it's so fast, then let me take the wheel,' she says. 'I've driven NASCAR at Daytona and Charlotte, so this should be a walk in the park.' Shit, I've never met a woman who has done Richard Petty School, and those fuck-me eyes knocked me off balance. 'Okay,' I say, being a wise ass. 'But if you see a cop, you're paying the speeding ticket.'

"Millie hops out of the car, and we meet by the hood. Damn, if she doesn't push me back on it and start kissing me like a prom-night virgin, massaging my crotch with her right hand. 'Just wanted you to see how I handle a gear shift,' she says in this low Marlboro voice.

"Then she giggles and bounces to the driver's side, and we both strap in. 'Hang on, big boy,' she says. Millie pops the clutch, and we peel out. That girl drives like Jeff Gordon. She had the Mac up to a hundred and a half in less than a minute, shifting the tranny right at the red line on the tach like we're at Le Mans."

Eddie paused to suck in some air. "Damned if she doesn't take us to the double century mark. Shit. I've never done that. Most women pee their pants at one and a quarter. Millie starts singing Beach Boy lyrics. 'If she had a set of wings, then I know she could fly.' I'm getting a boner just watching her.

"That's when she sees the blue gum balls in the rear-view mirror. 'Well,' she says as if someone just gave her a birthday present, 'Gendarmes. Do you think they got a make on our plates when I flew past them back there?'

"I look back, and there are not one but two cop cars

after us. We're going so goddamned fast that they're getting smaller by the second.

"'It's okay, baby,' I say. 'Just pull over up there, and I'll pay the ticket.'

"'The hell you will,' she says. 'This is go-to-jail. Go directly to jail. Do not pass go. Do not collect two hundred dollars stuff. Hang on; there's a turn up ahead.'

"She cuts the lights, downshifts to save the pads until the last minute, then slams the brakes, and we barely keep the Mac on the road as she takes the turn.

"By now, I'm just holding on for dear life as she punches the Mac again. But the cops have eagle eyes and saw us make the turn, even with no lights.

"Millie floors the gas pedal, screaming like we're on a ride at Disney. 'Catch us if you can, boys!' She slides into another turn and skids us into the driveway of some farmhouse, pulling a 360 so the nose is pointed toward the road.

"The first cop car shoots by us, sirens screaming. But the second guy is going slower and sees the dust from our skid. He inches into the drive until we are nose to nose. 'Damn,' Millie says. 'It's just one guy. I was hoping for two.' And I'm wondering what in the hell she means by that."

By now, I'm about to piss my pants. "I know exactly what she means by that."

Ed's not listening. "Anyway, the guy comes up to the driver's side window. Millie rolls it down and gives him this huge smile. 'Hey, Dave,' she purrs. 'Out chasing speeders tonight?'

"The cop rolls his eyes. 'Carol?' he says as if he just caught his sister with her hands in the cookie jar. 'What the hell are you doing?'

"I'm thinking, 'Who the hell is Carol?' She crosses her

arms on the open window so her boobs can rest on top and tilts her head, still smiling like he's a lunchroom monitor and not somebody who can throw her ass in jail.

"'Just seeing how fast this thing can go,' she says. 'Want to take it for a spin and see what you can do with it?'

"The cop shakes his head. 'No. I do not. You're lucky we didn't see the plates and call it in, or I'd have to arrest you.'

"'I bet I could talk you out of it,' she says. The cop turns tail and goes back to his car. 'No more speeding on the way home, Carol,' he yells. 'I mean it!' And then he pulls out of the drive and takes off after his buddy.

"Millie sighs. 'Who is Carol?' I ask. She leans over and plants another one on my lips and whispers, 'It's my pen-name. I write books about sex. Want to come to my place and I'll show you my research?'"

"Let me guess," I said. "She took you home and showed you her research."

I could hear the shivers in Ed's breath. "Oh, she showed me all right. When did you first decide you were in love with Patty?"

"Eddie, I'm divorced. You're asking a guy with horrible judgment."

"I think Millie could make me a one-man-woman."

I could feel the hair rise on the back of my neck. "She's not a one-woman-man, partner."

"After last night, I don't care if she's doing it with the pool boy. That woman fucks like a professional."

I hadn't met Mallory's best friend until the previous night. But "stay away" alarm bells started ringing in my head the moment she pinched Ed's ass at the Maracaibo.

"'No strings attached, lover boy,' she said as I limped out of her house about fifteen minutes ago. 'But whenever you need a date, I'll give you a great rate.'"

There was heart trouble in Ed's family. I began to think that he was lucky to have escaped Millie with his life.

"I think I'm in love, Andy. Can you imagine coming home to that every night?"

Nightmares were forming. "I can. And as your best friend, I'm telling you, don't walk. Run away from that woman."

"I've gotta go, Andy. I'm super late for this call. Talk to Mallory for me. See what Millie thought about me."

I was indignant. "I will not. Millie makes Patty seem like Mother Theresa. This is one disaster that you're going to have to manage yourself."

"At least see what Mal thinks, okay buddy? You're the best. And great job last night. I knew you'd come through for me."

"If you're seriously thinking about pursuing this psychopath, Eddie, have your lawyers look at every life insurance policy you own and make me the beneficiary."

"You're the best friend I guy could ever have, Andy. Call me after five and report."

The line went dead. It wasn't even eight in the morning and I already wanted a drink.

CHAPTER EIGHTEEN

M ALLORY

It was Trent who challenged us. He had some connection with the city, and I guessed that fact that Millie's business was immune from police harassment had something to do with him. He reminded us a bit about Fat Freddie, but I had learned that what was on the outside rarely reflected what was on the inside.

Everyone probably thinks about a same-sex encounter at some point in their lives. I explored it in high school. But while kissing a girl was definitely interesting, fucking a boy was so much more fun.

There was still time on the clock after Millie and I ravished Trent. He fell back into a recliner she had in her master suite, wheezing through nicotine-caked lungs that always gave our encounters a smoke-shop bouquet.

"Okay, ladies. Let's see some lesbian action... If that's part of Donna's 'rules of engagement.'"

This took us both aback. It was never something we had considered. After some extensive non-verbal eye contact, we both shrugged our shoulders and did it.

I thought about what great friends Millie and I had been. How we were there for one another through high school and college, through the darkest hours of our divorces, and how she had reassured me during the scary first months when we were adjusting to Ella's Down syndrome diagnosis. I thought about how few real friends we truly have in life and imagined expressing my gratitude as if Millie were a man.

As we knelt on the bed, studying one another, a new aura surrounded her. My best friend carried enough extra weight to be classified as a "BBW," a big beautiful woman in porno speak. Her curves had a little more insulation on them. She carried what we both jokingly called a "muffin" around her waist. Her tits were a pair of beautiful bulbous orbs with thick, rich areolae and tiny nipples that quickly hardened into sharp points when she was aroused.

To me, Millie was suddenly incredibly attractive and appealing. I felt a tingle in my pussy as we both leaned in and began to kiss.

The press of our breasts against one another and the sensation of our exploring hands was a huge turn-on.

I could see why Millie did so well with her clients. Her skills in the art of love were incredible. And since we were both women, we knew the details of our physiology much more intimately than any man ever could.

Millie took my tits into her hands as we continued to kiss with a passion that I thought surprised us both. Her thumbs circled my nipples with a perfect pressure that transmitted lightning bolts directly to my nether regions.

I returned the favor. Millie's areolae were particularly sensitive erogenous zones. She caught her breath when she felt my touch. Her eyes widened, and her expression transformed into unbounded desire.

Pressing me backward so I lay flat on the mattress,

Millie parted my legs and began to massage my clit with a breast. Her eye contact radiated affection and fun. She was loving this!

I understood that this was primarily a show for our customer and began to moan, closing my eyes and thrashing with each swipe of her wonderfully pointed nipples against my love button.

My performance energized my partner, too, and she dipped her head down to eat me out.

Most men have no idea about the extent of the sensitive areas around a woman's pussy. But girls know the geography by heart.

Millie's expert tongue had me moaning for real. Her fingers worked their magic inside of my slit, and I began to involuntarily swivel my hips in response.

But it was her practiced words that did it.

"Come for us baby. Show us what it's like to lose control!"

It wasn't an act. It was delightful and dirty and fulfilling. And I wanted to return the favor.

Millie slid open a drawer on the nightstand where she kept the tools of her trade. Beneath the condoms and next to the Hitachi vibrator was something I had never seen before: a two-headed, purple plastic cock.

Apparently, my friend had been holding out on me about a few more of her own adventures in sexuality.

Maintaining my position, I lubed up the phallus and slowly slid my half inside of my pussy.

I heard a grunt coming from Trent's direction and looked over to see him stroking his cock in response.

We knew the look when a customer was getting more than his money's worth. I began to think about how I would be spending my tip.

"Your turn," I said in my best husky voice. "Ride me until you come."

Millie giggled and straddled my body. She playfully circled her hands in front of her like an Arabian belly dancer as I held the rubber cock in position.

It takes a little practice, but two women can have a pretty sensual experience fucking with a double-sided dick. Millie and I quickly found our center, and she began to ride me like I had seen her do with our male clients.

Her pendulous breasts bounced up and down and she tossed her head back in unabated joy.

I couldn't tell if it was real at first, but I knew when she was in the zone, and as her pace quickened and the juices flowed out of her pussy and onto mine, I knew this was the real deal. She was nearing the summit.

So was Trent. He was beyond grunts, openly exclaiming, "Oh my God! Oh my God!" as he stroked himself faster and faster.

Millie raised an eyebrow in his direction, wordlessly letting me know that she was holding back until he came.

Trent did so. He hadn't thought about preparation for his output and had a moment of terror before grabbing a washcloth that Millie always kept within reach to capture his pulsing ejaculations.

Millie laughed, further increasing her tempo until her own climax engulfed her. My partner fell backward onto the bed. Both of us were now spread eagle, the double dildo still connecting us in a purple semi-circle as we panted with pleasure.

Millie looked at the clock. "Time's up," she gasped.

"Thank God," Trent wheezed. "You guys are gonna give me a heart attack."

"How much of that was an act?" I asked Millie as we prepared for our next customer."

"Some was," she said, pinching my ass. "But most of it wasn't."

"You know something, girlfriend," I said. "I don't consider myself a same-sex enthusiast but making love to you was a religious experience." I winked. "I'd do it again...off the clock."

I could see in Millie's eyes that the feeling was mutual. "We're both going straight to hell."

"How are things with the boyfriend?" I wondered. "How does he feel about your job now that he's in the picture?"

"I am who I am," Millie answered. "I can be emotionally exclusive and physically promiscuous. I'm a highly experienced professional who loves my job. The right guy should respect and admire that."

I wasn't so sure. "I don't know, girlfriend. We're getting into pretty thin moral ground here."

"Morals are what judgmental people use to justify their own hang-ups. I furnished my new master bedroom with the money I got from fucking an evangelist. The way he was talking to God as I sucked him off was a lot different than the fire and brimstone he throws at his congregation on Sundays."

I shook my head. "He'll have a hot time in the front office when it's his turn to negotiate with St. Peter."

Millie's tone softened. "Look, Mal, we are put on this earth to alleviate suffering. That's the essence of every religious practice since time began. I don't believe that God gives a shit how we do it, so long as nobody gets hurt in the process. He would be the first to say that some churches have totally bent his teachings to get people to do their bidding."

I couldn't stifle a smile. "I've never heard anything that heavy come out of your mouth before, Millie. When did you become a philosopher?"

"The day I fucked the mayor and he wanted his wife to watch."

"Conservative Cal Calhoun?"

"The genuine article. You may have noticed that his political leanings are a little more to the center these days."

What my friend was saying felt right. We've hidden behind masks even before this damned pandemic, terrified that someone might see who we really are. I was treading down a potentially slippery path. Morality truly is defined in the eye of the beholder. I hoped that my compass wasn't spinning out of control.

"You truly are an amazing soul, Mills." I said it with admiration and meant every word.

We gave one another a quick kiss, something that had been part of our comings and goings for years. Now it felt different. I realized my relationship with my best female friend had morphed into something deeper, richer, more meaningful.

Then, the doorbell rang. Our next client had arrived.

———

LIFE WAS PRETTY GOOD. BUT THE PURITAN IMAGE I radiated at work made me uncomfortable sharing my side hustle with anyone, especially Andrew.

I could be a wiseass with the best of them. But as we all know, humor and bravado often shield a sensitive heart.

Mine could be easily broken.

Sensuality was one-dimensional when it was a transaction. There was still a big hole in that heart, and I wished I had the courage to see if Andrew could fill it.

So I was more than a little afraid when he called to ask if he could return the favor for helping him with Ed's angel investors. His own tentative voice was disarmingly cute. It felt like he was as nervous as I was.

"Hey, Mal. I've really enjoyed how well the HR project has gone for all concerned. Now that it's wrapping up, I wondered if you wanted to…" He paused. I knew what he must be thinking. But how to say it without sounding like he wanted a repeat of last time. "Um, I wondered if you wanted to get together to celebrate our success?"

"I would love that," I heard myself say in full HR director/actor mode. "Do you want to include the girls, or should I get a sitter so we can mask up and try some outside dining?"

"My two are coming up on the end of the school year and are pretty focused during the week. But I would love to see Ella again. I could do any weeknight but Wednesday."

Wednesdays were still "Church Night" in our hypocritical town. Was there a dimension of the man I didn't know about?

"I'm free this Friday evening if that works."

And, I thought, we won't have to worry if our adventures end up rolling over into Saturday again.

The relief in his tone was palpable. "Sounds great! Let me bring the food. Tell me what you like, and I'll get it custom-crafted."

CHAPTER NINETEEN

ANDREW

"So you want me to cook for your other girlfriend?"

Jillian wasn't really mad when I asked her if she could whip up a little extra food for me to share with Mal and Ella. By now, I knew when her voice telegraphed real anger or joking sarcasm.

"She's not my other girlfriend, *Doctor.*" I used that term to piss her off.

She demanded it at work but hated when I used it. "In fact, this will be our first causal meeting since you and I met at the emergency room."

"I know exactly what to cook for you two," Jillian said, her eyes darting back and forth as the culinary options danced in her head.

"Are you gonna tell her about us?"

That was the question. Could I?

———

MALLORY

Damn, Andrew looked good. We had both adapted to the pandemic life and found ways to get our exterior appearances looking sharp. With the extra money from my side-hustle, I could afford the wardrobe, and well-masked professionals took care of my hands and feet every week. The ten pandemic pounds I carried were gone. For the first time in a long time, I was pleased with my body. I put on my best face for him and wore a new white linen pant suit that gave Andrew a great view of the Victoria's Secret undergarments that highlighted my best professional features.

Andrew was balancing two huge aluminum pans that were somehow at the perfect temperature and radiated the aroma of Italian food...my favorite.

When he put them on the countertop in the kitchen, Ella jumped into his arms before I could. I let her shower him with kisses. I would have to wait my turn.

ANDREW

Damn, Mal looked good. She must have found some sort of fitness formula that she could do at home. Her body was "model perfect," and the smile that I had seen so often on screen was even warmer and inviting in real life.

I instantly wanted her.

But Ella got first dibs. We three laughed and talked through dinner. Ella's vocabulary was expanding, and she loved repeating what we said. That led to some laugh-out-loud moments as we fed her some borderline inappropriate things to say.

The night was comfortably warm, and there was time to take the girl for a walk to the park afterward.

She had mastered the slides and swing sets, and there were other age mates to play with. Mal and I turned her loose and settled into one of the broad adult swings placed strategically for parents to keep an eye on the action.

"Dinner was wonderful, Andrew," Mal gushed. "Where on earth did you get it?"

Well, here we go. I guess there's no turning back.

"Jillian made it for you. Apparently, you've told her about a few of your favorite things."

Mal giggled. "How about those fake tits?"

"How do you women know that stuff? I couldn't even tell under the white coat."

"She radiates 'cougar,' my friend. She would jump on you in a minute if you gave her an opening."

I shrugged. "I guess I kinda did. We ran into one another at the grocery store, of all places, before the two of you struck up your friendship. It turns out she is quite the cook, too."

Mal tilted her head down, raising her eyebrows, giving me one of those "tell me more" looks.

"You restored my confidence that night, Mal," I said honestly. "I guess that connected with Jillian. We've sort of had a thing going since then."

I couldn't read what was going on inside Mal's beautiful head. HR people are like that. "Sounds delightful," was all she said. "How is it going?"

I searched Mal's eyes as I answered. "My oldest calls her my 'fuck buddy.' I guess that's the term that the kids use for someone who shares a physical relationship without commitment or romance. My shrink says these kinds of things happen to us in these extraordinary times we're all living."

Mal's face was an enigma. "Does she please you?"

"That's the question," I said, totally knowing the

answer. "The sex is…" I looked around to see if any kid was within earshot. "The sex is great. And I think she likes the fact that I'm not intimidated by her intellect and position."

"But.." Mal prodded.

"But she's not you."

There. I realized it as I said it. Mal was the whole thing, mind, body, and spirit rolled into one amazing package. I pressed on. It was now or never.

"I'm glad that this work thing is wrapping up because I've been uncomfortable about taking our relationship further while we were business colleagues. My girls think the doctor is a nympho and I'm simply her boy toy. They call her Dr. Dick-Me."

Mallory's laughter seemed to break the ice. It felt like a burden was lifting off my shoulders.

"I could have told you that the first time she inspected that sexy ass of yours in the ER."

"You're not mad?"

"I don't have that right," Mal said, her eyes sparkling in a way that melted my inhibitions. "We're not married. This is the first time we've really let our guards down to talk about what 'us' might mean."

Mal paused and swallowed. She suddenly seemed afraid. "And you're not the only one who has been playing the field."

CHAPTER TWENTY

M

ALLORY

I had to admit that hearing Andrew talk about Jillian made me jealous. But I meant what I said. We weren't a thing. He was free to do whatever he wanted. The question was: What did I want him to do?

I knew that his ex had been cheating on him for over a year before their breakup. So if a relationship was going to work, trust would be paramount. How much should I share?

I felt like that guy in *Animal House* who had the angel on one shoulder and the devil on the other. One part of me was embarrassed to tell him that I was essentially a prostitute. Another part of me knew that we couldn't take another step toward an understanding if he didn't know the truth.

I didn't know any way to couch it, so I just blurted it out.

"I'm having sex five to ten times a week, and I get a thousand dollars an hour for my trouble."

Andrew's expression was confusion. Was I being a smart ass in response to his honesty?

"Millie has an escort business. Basically, she and I are high-class hookers. She's Donna and I'm Gina. She roped me into a threesome soon after the exquisite night you and I shared together." I had to pause to catch my breath as that memory poured over me. "I was vulnerable because after being with you, I wanted more love. So, I did it. It turns out I'm good at it, and the thing kind of progressed from there. I have anywhere from eighteen to twenty-four clients. It's not always about the sex. Some just want the company. The common denominator is that they are rich and can afford to treat me well. I try to give them their money's worth."

I felt like I had just barfed out the delicious dinner we had just eaten. For the first time since I started fucking for money, I felt ashamed.

Andrew's face morphed through a half dozen different emotions as I spilled my guts.

When he spoke, it was just three words. His expression was non-judgmental. But I wondered if his words were.

"Are you happy?"

ANDREW

Holy shit! This perfect woman wasn't so perfect after all. She was a whore! My head vectored to a picture of a dozen men fucking that beautiful pussy at once. I felt angry, resentful, hurt, and worried about her safety, all at the same time.

But I controlled it. I didn't think she knew what was going through my mind when I asked her if she was happy.

After processing all of my own emotions and peeling

away the selfishness, that was the only important question. It wasn't just about me. It was about her, too.

Mal started humming something, closing her eyes as if trying to conjure up a memory.

"What's that eighties song by *Extreme*? 'There's a hole in my heart that can only be filled by you.'" Mal held my hand between her two. "That sounds silly and stupid and hypocritical coming from a hooker, doesn't it? But I guess that's the bottom line."

She searched my eyes. Hers looked like they might be about to produce some tears. "Now that you know everything, what do you think?"

Mal let go of my hand and focused on Ella. Her girl was laughing as another munchkin pushed her on the grown-up swings.

"That's a dumb question. I just dumped this big hairy thing in your lap with no time to even process what it might mean."

She took a deep breath. "I'm feeling like I'm screwing up the best thing that might ever happen to me."

How *did* I feel? Did I want to demand exclusivity if we were to try to make a relationship work? That was the paradigm. The expectations of a controlling male culture.

I pondered her question to me. *What did I need?*

I thought I knew what needing her meant. Now I wasn't so sure.

"I guess we've given one another a lot to process," I finally said. "Nothing you've said dims my interest in the least. Yeah, the idea of other guys having their way with you is a little unnerving. But I'm basically doing the same thing."

Now it was my turn to take her hand in mine.

"But if total exclusivity was important to you, I would drop Jillian in a heartbeat to be with you."

CHAPTER TWENTY-ONE

MALLORY
When Ella was good and exhausted, Andrew picked her up and gave her a shoulder ride home.

We didn't say much on the way. I think the impassioned info dump on both sides was messing with our heads.

I was finding a unique fulfillment I had not expected as "Gina" and wasn't sure I was ready to give up the cash, nor the satisfaction that came with pleasing my clients.

Could I be emotionally exclusive with Andrew and still fuck other guys? How would we find out?

We both flipped the switch into parental mode when we got back to my place. It was a repeat of our first evening. Ella loved having Andrew cheering her on in the bathtub. We read a book to her together, and I let him take my daughter into her room at bedtime, watching him work his magic in the rocking chair.

"Daddy," she yawned.

There was that word again. It was the one thing no

therapist could ever be. It was the most important thing I wanted for my girl: a mother *and* a father.

In so many ways, Andrew was the man of my dreams. I felt myself getting wet for him. And I wanted to show him what I had learned on the job.

———

ANDREW

When I came out of Ella's bedroom, Mallory was waiting for me. She was still in the linen outfit, but the undergarments were gone. Her smile exuded love, and I watched as her nipples stiffened as she took my measure. She slid a pair of fingers into her pants, massaging on either side of her clit in an up and down motion that instantly made me hard.

The contrast between Mallory and Jillian clarified like a fog lifting. I was falling in love with Mal, with her kid, with the amazing professionalism she brought to work every day, with that smart-ass sense of humor, and with the vulnerable, imperfect heart that beat inside that perfect body.

In guy-speak, sex with Jillian was like masturbating to really great porn. Intimacy with Mal was making love.

———

MALLORY

I was so ready for Andrew to fuck me. The finger stuff was totally for his benefit, and I was pleased to see that, despite the astonishing revelations at the park, he was still interested.

I wasn't really jealous of Jillian. So what if she took care of his needs in that area? Wasn't that what I was doing?

Was I rationalizing? Would I wake up in the morning hating him? Hating myself?

I thought about the latest Covid numbers the news was reporting. We both had friends who had died or were dying. Tomorrow was uncertain, let alone the long life we might want to share. As long as we both knew who owned our hearts, wasn't that what was most important right now?

I led him to the bedroom, set the lighting low, and hit the button on the new sound system I could now afford, starting up a new age playlist that whispered to us like the soundtrack at a spa.

We faced one another at the foot of the bed. I began to undress him, nodding to the buttons on my top, inviting him to do the same.

As the last of our clothing fell away, we stood, naked and ready, making a memory. Andrew's body had not put on an ounce of fat during the past six months. I guess I owed Jillian some thanks for that. His fully erect cock pulsed, a drop of precum already evident on the tip.

"I've picked up a few new skills since last time," I purred.

Andrew framed my face with his hands.

"I think tonight, I'm feeling like I want old-school," he said as he pulled me to his waiting mouth.

Andrew's kisses began as light brushes against my lips. He circled my nose with his before tilting my head, ever so slightly so our tongues could explore one another.

The psychic impact was something I didn't expect. I began to cry. Tears streamed down my face, and I broke our kiss.

"I feel like this sex worker thing is the biggest mistake of my life. Have I let you down?"

Andrew smiled at me. He smiled! He lifted me up as if

he were carrying me across the threshold, the threshold of a new understanding, gently laying me on the mattress.

As I looked up at him, he spread my legs, guiding that beautiful cock toward my wet, waiting pussy.

Andrew paused after inserting the tip, pulling back out and massaging my clit with the head of his dick. His eyes never left mine. I could feel the emotions flying between us. My tears continued to roll down my cheeks, even as I felt my body shiver toward orgasm.

"It's okay, Mal," Andrew said, his voice soft and comforting. "This is the difference between what we do for others and what we can only do for one another."

Andrew slowly entered me until we were fully one. He wrapped his arms around me, pressing his chest against my own as he kissed me.

I came like a skyrocket.

CHAPTER TWENTY-TWO

ANDREW

We do what we must to get through life's complicated moments. I couldn't reject Mallory on the spot. My own physical desire for her was still volcanic. But, I'd admit that the escort thing bothered me. I needed to peel back the onion to understand whether or not I could be exclusive with someone who wasn't really exclusive with me.

"Love is a rare mixture," I remembered my dad explaining in our 'Birds and the Bees' talk. "We humans didn't always live as long as we do now. Back in the age of knights and dragons, kids your age were thrust into arranged marriages. Girls had babies at age sixteen because you didn't know if you would live to be twenty. Evolution programmed us guys to create as many more of us as we could as quickly as possible because a lot of babies didn't make it back then."

I could hear my mother's yell from another part of the house. "Honey! How many times have I told you *not* to leave your coat on the couch? Hang the thing up. That's what closets are for. You're as bad as the children!"

My dad smiled one of those "I'm guilty" smiles I knew well. "Over the generations, we started to live longer, and the mating dance got more complicated. We had to have connections that were more than just physical. God gave us all hearts and hearts are easily broken. And…" he paused for effect, "we all have our imperfections." He shot a glance at the doorway, hoping, I thought, that Mom wasn't in earshot. "Love is about deciding what you'll put up with. Make sure that whoever you finally choose has enough check marks on the plus side to offset any that might slide over to the negative side as the years go by."

Was Mal's new side hustle a negative or a positive?

I needed to know more, so I scheduled lunch with Millie.

———

"So Mal came clean, eh?"

I had to admit, Millie looked terrific. Nature gave her more ballast, and she would never be considered model material by today's anorexic standards. But she knew how to accentuate the positive, and her eyes radiated a playful glow that I imagined made her clients instantly erect.

"She gave me a pretty good overview of the escort business. I'm not sure I'd buy that mutual fund, but it sounds like her investments are generating the returns she wants."

"You guys," Millie laughed. "It's either euphemisms or monosyllables. Mal is very good at what she does in every part of her life. As a sex worker, she has few equals."

I could imagine.

"So, big boy, how do you feel about it?"

"That's kind of why I'm here, Mil. I'm not sure. My

traditional upbringing is clashing with evolving twenty-first-century values."

Millie pulled a small piece of cork out of her wine glass. "The best thing Congress could do is legalize weed and sex work. We'd all be so tired and chill that crime rates would go down and world peace would ensue."

"Love conquers all?"

"Exactly. So what do you need to know to decide whether or not you can fall in love with a whore?"

"Geeze, Millie! I hate that word. I associate it with slavery, human trafficking, all of the bad things that can be connected with sex work."

"Whore… *We Have Outstanding Relationship Experiences*. That's how I define it. I know more about what's inside a man's head than most women ever will. They think they're paying me for sex, but what they really want is someone to listen without judgment, someone who isn't a 'significant other' to ask them the tough questions, someone they can try on different personalities with until they find that person they were born to be."

"I'd like to believe that," I said. "But I think it's a little more complicated."

Millie sipped her wine. I knew from experience with Jillian's stash that it cost twenty-five dollars a glass. "Of course it is, dummy! Nothing worth pursuing in this life is easy." She pointed a finger at me. "Especially that soulmate we all seek."

That reminded me of something Mal had said. "Speaking of soulmates. How goes it with your own Mr. Wonderful."

Millie sighed. "Didn't work out. But it wasn't my job that ended it. The older we get, the more particular we are. He turned out to be a little too needy. I've lived that life and like guys who respect my independence."

Wow. This was a different woman from the insecure, body-shaming girl Mallory had described in college. Dad was right. People evolve. I'd have to bring that one up with my shrink. It scared me.

Millie saw my fingers tapping on the tablecloth and put a hand over mine to calm them. "Look, Andy. We're living in a wartime world. This fucking Covid thing will ultimately kill and maim more people than all of our wars combined. Tomorrow is never guaranteed. What's that cliché? 'Plan as if you would live forever, but live as if you might die tomorrow?' If this thing you and Mal have feels right, just let it happen. Every day is a gift. Don't waste a single one. Deal with the land mines when and if they appear."

"How did you get so smart?" I asked Mallory's best friend.

"Experience. I spent too much of my life being angry about who I couldn't be and missed out on what I could become."

Millie brought her glass to her mouth, pausing to look at me over the top of it. "Did she tell you about us?"

I thought that this was what the lunch was all about.

Millie saw my confusion. She flashed me a weird, dirty smile. "How do you feel about bi-sexuality?"

CHAPTER TWENTY-THREE

MALLORY

Andrew invited Ella and me over for a swim with his girls, and I accepted. Dana and Dani were smitten with my miracle girl, and she was over the moon to see them again. The three suited up, and we could soon hear splashing and laughter coming from the pool.

Andrew and I were both relaxed and well-lubricated by a few Moscow Mules. I had some questions, and the alcohol made them easier to ask.

"Did you have anything to do with Doctor J's outreach?"

We were calling Jillian Dr. J. at our house.

Andrew couldn't hide the smile. "All I did was encourage the connection. It sounds like you two have taken it beyond the examination room."

"I can't believe that she's a crazy woman in the bedroom," I said. "At work, she's professional, caring, compassionate, and totally loves Ella."

"Who wouldn't love Ella?"

"It's just weird that she doesn't want kids of her own or the benefits of a soulmate."

The slider opened, and the three kids came running through the room. Dani had Ella in her arms, and my kid was pressing the trigger of a battery-powered squirt gun. Dana was dodging the streams as they circled the sectional where Andrew and I sat.

He didn't seem to mind that chlorinated water was stripeing his carpet and furniture.

With another whoop, the girls disappeared back out to the pool deck, and we could hear a splash as they jumped into the water.

Andrew's look transmitted the irony. "Maybe, Jillian likes the fact that she can have the kid experience on her terms. For you, it's 24/7."

"And you, *Dad*," I emphasized the Dad part. "You've got two girls. What's that disgusting saying? 'When you have a son, you only have to worry about one dick. When you have a daughter, you worry about every dick."

Andrew knew the reference. "I decided long ago that all I could do was model the behavior for my kids and hope they grew up at least knowing my definition of right and wrong."

I nodded toward the pool. "You seem to be doing a great job."

Andrew sniffed. "Far from it. At least they know I love them, no matter what they do. Maybe they will do a better job at picking a partner than I did."

"Patty? What went wrong?"

Andrew frowned in mock affront. "Aren't we asking the personal questions today?"

"You don't have to answer. I'll go first if that's easier. Elliot wanted this perfect family. When Ella was born with Down syndrome, that dream went up the chimney. I think he started looking at me with a more critical eye, as if that extra chromosome was my fault. In the end, he simply couldn't shoulder the burden of a flawed spouse and what he saw as a flawed kid."

Andrew glanced at the pictures of his girls on the fireplace mantle. He stuck a wallet-sized copy of Ella's pre-kindergarten portrait into the edge of one of the frames.

"He does not know how perfect Ella truly is." Andrew's gaze turned wistful. "I wonder how Patty would have approached that adventure."

Andrew took a deep breath. I knew that if I waited, the story would come.

"Patty and I have known one another since high school. We were both jocks. I guess that was the first thing we had in common. And we hated each other initially. You know how those adolescent hormones work. You carry grudges over meaningless slights. And you see anybody else who shares what you think are your special gifts as competition."

"She could outrun you?"

Andrew laughed. "In the farm town I came from, that was the definition of a virgin. A girl who could outrun her boyfriend. Imagine how that joke would go over in today's MeToo world."

"So, Patty was a virgin when you got together?"

"You're rushing the story, Mal."

I took another swig of my mule and rested my chin on a palm. "Impatience is one of my many flaws. I'll shut up. Continue."

"There comes a time when everybody in school is screwing everybody else. It used to be a college thing in our parents' day. But I had to have the safe sex talk with Dani when she was ten. The whole thing disgusted her. 'I already know about that, Dad! Dana told me everything. And no boy is touching me without my permission, or I'll kick him in the balls!'"

"Smart girl," I murmured.

"Well, Aphrodite made her appearance, and suddenly, this athletic girl with the firecracker personality looked pretty delicious. She busted my cherry after a football game, and I was pretty much into her pants from then on."

"And the feeling was mutual?"

"Not all the time. I wasn't Patty's first. I should have figured that out when she sucked the chrome off of my trailer hitch. She obviously had coaches who taught her well."

I thought about "Mal and Mil," the moniker Millie and I had in college. My own knowledge of the art was enhanced by a half dozen helpful young men who weren't afraid to tell me what "made Winkie sing."

"We would break up for a while and fuck other people. But we always got back together. Everyone in school just assumed we were meant for each other."

I was doing the math in my head. Dana was sixteen. Andrew was married for seventeen years. He was thirty-six. That meant his first kid was born when he was nineteen.

"So you made it through one year of college and then your birth control failed?"

"I wish we were that smart. She was a physical education major, and I was a business guy. Of course, we went to the same college, and our break-up and make-up pattern continued. During a period where we were split up, we ran into one another at the bar where our friends hung out. We were both the worse for alcohol consumption. I apologized to her for something I probably didn't do, and she told me to fuck off. I went back to my dorm room, deciding that this co-dependent thing we had would not

117

work, and went to sleep determined to put her out of my mind."

"I can see it coming," I said. "Patty had second thoughts about her blow up at the bar."

"'Coming' is the operative word. Yup. So I'm sleeping and having this exquisite dream about getting a world-class blow job, and I wake up to see that it's really happening to me, and Patty is doing the sucking. You know what happens when someone learns your sexual triggers."

I knew. And the trigger man was sitting next to me.

"She gets me so hard that it's hurting and then rips off her undies and slips it in. I kept throwing condoms at her, and she kept dodging them, saying, 'Fuck me, I'm not ovulating yet, and I want to feel your jizz power wash my cervix.'"

Andrew rolled his eyes. "She wasn't going to stop until I did as I was told, and finally, I couldn't hold back any longer."

Andrew took a long drink of his mule.

"She was ovulating all right. That little egg turned out to be Dana, nine months later, to the day."

"So you did the honorable thing and married her?"

"I've always done the honorable thing. Talk about a double-edged sword. Sometimes the best thing you can do for a person is be dis-honorable."

"And Patty never lost her wanderlust?"

Andrew nodded sadly. "People don't change. We think we can change them, but you either accept them as they are, or you move on. I tried to accept Patty's issues. We had some good times between the bad. But I guess I knew all along that she would stray again."

That surprised me. "Again?"

"Yeah. There were several other guys. I always found

out about them. But it wasn't until this last one that Patty decided the problem was me and not her."

I couldn't resist rolling my tongue in a circle to moisten the lips I hoped Andrew would be kissing before the day was done. "I can't imagine you being the problem."

"I'm a provider. Patty wanted a plaything. I knew that in high school. But she was also world-class in the bedroom, a regular bucking bronco. Sex was the ultimate affirmation for an insecure guy."

I was incredulous. "You seem to have your shit pretty well together for an insecure guy."

"I'm a good actor. It took a lot of therapy for me to realize that what I needed was the emotional connection."

I now had the perfect setup to ask the question I really wanted to be answered. "So why Jillian? Isn't she just another Patty in a white lab coat?"

Andrew leaned back against the sofa and looked at the ceiling. "Old habits die hard. I'm a sap. A rescuer. Why do you think I ended up in human resources? But what's different about Jillian is that we both know there is nothing beyond the physical." Andrew shot a glance outside to make sure the kids couldn't hear us. "I may be rationalizing big time but knowing that I can blow off steam sexually one night every week in this crazy world we're dealing with has been helpful."

Andrew put his hand on my knees. That gaze that always lit me up locked with mine. "I care about you in ways I've never cared about anyone before. We seem to fit, not just sexually, but as this complete thing. It's as if all the puzzle pieces finally connect and the finished product is this thing of immense beauty that I never want to break up."

I felt a surge of wetness dampen my panties and pulled a pillow on my lap to hide it. "Jesus, Andrew. Don't talk like that when I can't jump on you and have my way. The girls are going to think I'm incontinent.

Andrew grinned. "Oh, my girls will know exactly what's going on. And I'll get the blame later."

Andrew's face softened. The mixture of affection and concern was irresistible. "Look, Mal. An important part of what makes that work is your happiness. If you want to continue this side hustle thing, do it. Hell, I don't care if you and Millie dance the lesbian two-step every other night. I think I can live with that. But we'll never know until we see what the day-to-day feels like. If you're willing to give this thing a try, so am I."

CHAPTER TWENTY-FOUR

ANDREW

I admit to being a little stunned when I saw Millie's caller ID pop up about the time I got home.

"Andrew! Can I come to see you?"

"What's happened, Millie. Are you okay?"

"I'm more than okay, but I need to make sure it's okay to be okay."

I had no idea what that meant but sighed and agreed to let Mal's best friend invade my peace and quiet.

She arrived in jeans and a typical Millie T-shirt that said, "Yeah, these are my boobs. Check out my eyes."

"If you're trying to stop men from objectifying you, Millie, I don't think that shirt is helping."

"Oh, I don't mind being objectified. It's very good for business. Are you going to let me stand on your front porch and ogle my curves, or are you going to invite me in?"

"My manners," I said, holding open the door. "It's a little late for me to imbibe, but can I get you a drink?"

"Vodka on the rocks," Millie said. "And bring the bottle."

She had a look in her eyes that set off warning bells inside my head.

"Let's set the boundaries right now, Millie. I'm not touching Mallory's best friend in any inappropriate ways. Are we clear on that?"

"I'm not thinking of you, big boy," Millie said, downing a double vodka and refilling her place before the ice had a chance to melt. "I want to know about your boss."

———

IT TURNED OUT THAT MILLIE'S ONE ENCOUNTER WITH Eddie had lit both of their candles. Millie couldn't have cared less about my friend's wealth and position. His ADD fascination with everything and everyone turned her on. And her total disregard for his achievements drew him to her like a bee to honey.

"You know what I do for a living, Andrew," she said as her liquor began to work. "Do you think Eddie will dump me if I tell him?"

"We both had pretty liberal attitudes in college," I said. "And the way he responded to your act at the restaurant told me he doesn't mind embarrassment. Beyond that, I couldn't tell you. Guys often have double standards. I'm not sure Ed has *any* standards. Aside from being married to serial entrepreneurship, who knows what goes on in that head of his."

Millie's eyes glazed, and her gaze focused on infinity. "I think I'm falling in love."

"No, you're not. You're infatuated. You've never met a

guy like Ed, and he's knocked you off of your center. You two don't know one another well enough to recognize what love might look like yet."

Millie took another dose of her vodka. "If he were here, I'd suck him off right in front of you. Would he find that a little over the top?"

"*I* find that a lot over the top, madam," I said. "But there are many areas where my best friend and I diverge. When he got crazy, he would dance naked in a public fountain and not care if the NASDAQ board saw him do it."

"Oh," Millie said, a shiver of anticipation running through her. "That's the man for me. I needed confirmation of his character before deciding what to do about it."

"Mal has worked for Ed for years, Millie. Why didn't you ask her?"

"She only knows the work guy. I have known him in the biblical sense. And oh, how that man loves to dash in where angels fear to tread."

I held up a hand. "No details, please. I witnessed enough of his debauchery in college."

"Then you'd bless our pairing?" Millie asked.

I thought for a moment. "Let's say I would not be surprised by your paring. Whether the two of you help one another become better people or not is an open question."

Millie bounced to her feet, skipping toward my front door. "That' just what I hoped to hear, Andrew."

I followed her, wondering if she planned to drive home with an open bottle of booze and an elevated blood alcohol content.

At the door, she wrapped her arms around my neck, bottle and glass still in hands, and kissed me as if we had just known each other in the biblical sense.

"You're the best, Andrew. I can see why Mel likes you. And one of these days, I *will* fuck you. So be prepared."

With that, Millie bounced out the door and into the cool of the evening.

CHAPTER TWENTY-FIVE

MALLORY

There's always a moment of tension when you first meet a new client. This one had come highly recommended from another one Millie and I trusted.

So, I wasn't ready for the face that greeted me at her door.

"Hello 'Gina.' Remember me?"

Elliot.

I was instantly angry. "What are you doing here?"

"I heard from a friend on the city council about his amazing woman and decided to see for myself what he was raving about."

"So you got a friend to vet himself and took his place?"

"Still as smart as ever. Aren't you going to invite me in?"

I stood my ground. "What do you want, Elliot?"

"Just interested to see if the mother of my child has learned any new skills since I last fucked her."

This wasn't the man I thought I knew. He radiated evil.

"You're about four months past due on your alimony payments, Elliot. I thought business was bad."

"It is. And I'm lonely. Angel and I have been struggling. She wants more children. I don't. She's, how can I put this delicately, withholding her charms. And you're right. I'm deep into my nest egg trying to keep things afloat. So I thought we could work out a trade."

I pressed my ex two steps backward and stepped out onto the front porch. The sound of the electronic door lock clicking was both reassuring and frightening. He wasn't getting inside where he could hurt Millie. But I was alone with a man I realized I didn't know at all.

"You're married, Elliot. What are you talking about?"

"Oh, it's a win-win, sweetheart. You take care of me." He rubbed my nose with a fat thumb. "And you get to keep Ella."

That lit me up. My mom protectiveness kicked in, and I zeroed in on where I might kick this asshole where it would hurt the most.

"The divorce decree says she's mine. You signed it."

"Oh, I don't want Ella," Elliot's voice was dead calm, menacing. "But I think a judge I know will agree that a foster home is a better place for a special needs kid than living with a whore."

Tears of anger welled up. "Why are you doing this? Why would you hurt an innocent child just to get back at me?"

Elliot feigned innocence. "All I want is a little love." He backed me up against the door. I could smell alcohol on his breath. "No commitment, 'Gina.' Just a mutually beneficial exchange of value."

His hand lightly squeezed my neck. "How about it? I've heard your blow jobs are world-class."

CHAPTER TWENTY-SIX

A NDREW
Seeing Mal's caller ID quickened my heart rate. The memory of what followed our family afternoon was still fresh. My girls took Ella back to Mallory's place, leaving us to continue unpacking years of sorrow and shame in my bedroom. It was something I hoped would become a habit. We might not be in love just yet, but every indicator was pointing in that direction.

"I need to see you right now." The voice didn't sound like it was another spider bite. It bordered on terror.

"What's wrong?"

"Get over here as fast as you can."

———

MALLORY
I told Andrew everything. Elliot's threats. The disgusting look on his face as he dropped his pants. The filthy taste that made me gag. And his vile grin as he said,

"That was a pleasant start. We'll work on those skills again next week."

"This whole thing was a huge mistake, Andrew. And now I'm trapped. I know Elliot will do what he promised. I'm lost."

———

ANDREW

I wanted to kill the guy then and there. You know the feeling when your anger controls you and you don't care what happens? That was where I was. I thought of a dozen ways to dispatch that bastard to the fires of hell.

But that wouldn't help Mallory. If anything happened to her ex-husband, her own story would get out. The possibility of losing Ella was very real.

And even if I had nothing to do with it, people around us were seeing Mal and me as a couple. They would make connections. Bad things would happen.

I needed time to think and a person to bounce this horrific mess off of.

———

"You know something, cowboy?"

Jillian poured us two glasses of her most expensive red wine.

"This might be the first time you walk out of my house without getting laid."

"It's a royal cluster fuck," I muttered, taking the glass from her hand and sucking down the medication.

Jillian slid into a recliner across from me. I appreciated the social distance. Today I needed her brain and not her body.

"When you are a respected physician with my unique proclivities, eventually someone crosses your path who will try to take advantage of you."

I tried to listen but couldn't get Mal's devastated face out of my mind.

"It was about three years ago when I had my own brief encounter with an opportunist."

That perked me up.

"A cheating husband. He brought his kid into the ER with an acute case of poison ivy and decided I was going to be his next conquest."

Jillian winced and took a dose of the wine. "I didn't do my homework. He said he was divorced, and it wasn't until we had a month of hay romping in the books that I found out he wasn't."

"What did you do?"

"I told him it was over. And he told me it wasn't. 'If you dump me, I'll spread the word about your perversions and you'll never treat another child again.'"

Jillian closed her eyes and sniffed the bouquet of the exquisite red. "People underestimate the medicinal value of a good glass of wine."

My impatience was boiling over. "So... What happened?"

"Tell you what, Andrew. It's better if you and Mal don't know. Let me do a little homework with Miss Millie. I think we have some interesting options."

That wouldn't work for me. Whatever happened, I was going to be invested in it.

"Nope. It's all of us or nothing, Jillian. And I don't like the idea of you putting your career at risk for a fuck buddy."

That day I saw a third type of smile on Jillian's face. I knew about the smiles she gave me when we talked shop.

And the way her mouth twisted on one side when I tickled her coital appetite was smile number two.

This one was different. Her eyes radiated empathy. The curves of her lips bent upward just enough to express the subtle affection I was learning to connect with genuine affection. Perhaps this woman was capable of more than physical connections after all.

"Okay, babe." It was the first time she had called me "babe."

"We're all in this together. Gather the troops, and let's make this ex-husband wish he had never been born with a dick."

CHAPTER TWENTY-SEVEN

NDREW

Here's the 411 on Elliot Michaels. College grad in advertising and public relations. Internship with the GainStrive Agency that led to a full-time gig. Such was his success that he and a partner bought the firm from retiring owners, rebranding it as GainStrive/Michaels.

He and Mal had a seven-year engagement before tying the knot. Apparently, Elliot's hunger for closing the sale crossed over into conquests outside of the office. Mal broke off the engagement several times. But Elliot's sales skills ultimately won the day.

His philandering heart gave Jillian the opening she was looking for, and she footed the bill to hire a private investigator to dig deep into both Elliot's and Mallory's backgrounds to see what opportunities and risks might bubble up.

His second wife was the polar opposite of Mallory, a controlling personality who wanted an All-American household with kids running around and family dinners on schedule at 6 pm every night. Elliot preferred the "Mad Men" lifestyle. The possibility of another imperfect child terrified him. That definitely strained their relationship. I suspected Elliot was finding what was missing elsewhere.

Millie's contribution was the installation of a camera system in the master suite where Mal conducted her business. She instructed "Gina" carefully, and the video record painted a, shall we say, "unflattering" picture of a predator who used threats to get sexual favors from his ex-wife.

The process took time, and that took a toll on all of us. The thought of that slime ball touching Mallory made me want to break every bone in his body. Mal's own psychological state was precarious, and I could sense her pulling back as the PTSD piled on.

When everyone agreed we had our ducks in a row, Mallory called her attorney. Ted Brannigan wasn't the sharpest tack in the drawer, but the package we gave him was more than enough to get the job done.

Jillian's plan of action was brilliant. But it all depended on one person who wasn't on our team.

———

MALLORY

Elliot's kinks became more and more disgusting. There was a period where I felt so helpless that I thought of giving everything up and moving to a different state with my girl.

But as our plan gelled, I felt my power returning. I went into character whenever Elliot showed up and what the camera recorded was a submissive victim with an undercurrent of anger and courage that would play well if a jury ever saw the scenes play out.

Ironically, my other clients continued to reinforce my self-confidence. I never said a word about my troubles. Customers don't care about that stuff. The balance shifted from bedroom activities to dinners and psychological support. Anyone who saw me out and about got the impression that I was a divorcee who was doing just fine in the male department, with many attentive friends and a positive attitude that attracted more.

But the most amazing person in all of this was Andrew. He now knew everything about me. The PI dug into the Mal and Mil years in college, created dossiers on every customer, along with a blow-by-blow account of the divorce. We had no secrets. He had a complete picture of this very imperfect woman. And all it did was make him care more deeply about me.

Andrew admitted he was a rescuer. But I saw him grow into a supporter. The experience taught him that sometimes he could be most valuable as a listener, a witness, asking clarifying questions and sharing multiple points of view, not all of which were that comfortable to hear.

We had been together long enough where the "personal assistants" we all send to relationships at the start fall away and the authentic person emerges. We had our fights. But we fought fair, and we both knew that the tension came from a place of love and admiration, not from selfishness and fear.

My challenges brought us closer, and the mutual growth that my shrink defined as healthy in committed relationships convinced us both that thing we had was developing into the best possible definition of love.

That love would soon be tested. Finally, the time came when we had what we needed. Jillian volunteered to make the approach. My man's fuck buddy was willing to put herself on the line for us. Our bond as friends deepened into mutual admiration and trust. As far as I was concerned, if she came through, she could have Andrew whenever she wanted him.

CHAPTER TWENTY-EIGHT

A NDREW
Here's Jillian's account of her meeting with Angel Michaels. I'll let her tell it in her own words.

———

AFTER YOU'VE BEEN A KID DOC LONG ENOUGH, YOU eventually get to know every parent in town. Angel and Elliot had trouble getting pregnant at first. So when Timothy Elliot Michaels was born, she was terrified of losing him and sought me out.

Timmy was a low-maintenance baby. Angel installed the SIDS alarms in his crib and was one of those over-cautious mothers I could see morphing into a bulldozer parent as Timmy grew.

So lunch with a patient's mom didn't ring any alarm bells at home. I had done a good job keeping my involvement with Andrew under the radar. As far as Elliot knew, this was just another of his high-maintenance wife's connections with the doctor who watched over their kid's health.

"Is age two appropriate for enrolling Timmy in a Montessori program?" Angel sipped her flavored soda water and picked at the salad in front of her. "I've read all the stuff on the internet, and there are things I can do at home, too."

We discussed the pros and cons for about twenty minutes before it occurred to Angel that this was the first time I had initiated a meeting. Her face darkened. When a doctor wants to see you, it's never good news.

"Listen to me. I've been blathering about nonsense and totally have forgotten that it was you who wanted to see me. Is Timmy okay? Did his latest blood work come back with a problem?"

That poor kid had been poked more times than a voodoo doll. Every time he sneezed, Angel wanted a full work-up.

I produced what I figured would be the last smile of the day. "You have one of the healthiest boys I've ever treated. I want to talk about you and Elliot."

Angel sighed. "I know, Doctor. We can be overbearing parents. I want the best for my baby boy, and you're the best doc in town. You need to tell me if I'm overstepping my bounds."

"That's not it, Angel." I pulled a thick folder out of my purse. "This has nothing to do with your parenting. Under normal circumstances, what I'm about to share with you would violate a dozen different privacy laws. But another patient asked me for advice and I felt I owed it to you to make you aware."

I slide the folder toward Angel. She regarded it as if it was a hot stove.

"It's about Elliot."

She knew. I nodded.

"He's always been a bit of a wild hair. But he's a good provider and an engaged dad. I want a bigger family. He doesn't. No marriage is perfect. And I realize I own my share of our issues."

I slowly shook my head and pointed to the folder. She needed to open it.

With the careful attention of a curator looking at a newly discovered archeological artifact, Angel pinched a tiny edge of the folder and flipped it open.

I could see the confusion in her eyes transmogrify into horror and then into anger. It was all there. Elliot's first encounter with Mallory at Millie's house. His threats. Transcripts of the videos.

And there was something else.

Angel choked on her words. "Who is Sherrie Jourdan?"

My voice was quiet, empathetic, but firm. "Turn the page."

An eight by ten color print of Elliot with his arm around a young redhead peered back at Angel. Her husband was nibbling on the girl's ear.

"Sherrie Jourdan is an associate at his firm, Angel."

Elliot's wife slid the photo to the side and read the PI's notes. When she came across the pertinent factoid, she gasped.

"She's pregnant?"

"I'm sorry, Angel. Your husband is blackmailing his ex-wife for sex and appears to be cheating on you. Mallory gave me this information. She didn't feel comfortable passing it on herself. But we both wanted you to be aware."

Tears of rage boiled in Angel's eyes. She pounded the table with her fists. Her voice sounded like the Wicked Witch of the West.

"I knew it. Business is terrible. Elliot told me he's had to travel to try to generate more."

I flipped a page for her, revealing a calendar print-out.

"Compare these dates. They always go to the same place."

Then Angel Michaels fell apart. With elbows on the table, her head sank into her hands, and she sobbed.

I've heard my share of crying. Doctors learn to share bad news with a gentle directness. The best of us tack on "I'm so sorry" to the end because the hurt rips out of a piece of our hearts, too.

Angel's sobs were different. Her eyes pressed shut as if opening them might make her head explode. I was grateful for social distancing and the table that was far from listening ears and prying eyes.

A server gave me a quizzical look, and I waved him away.

It took time. I watched Angel sprint through the Kübler-Ross continuum. She was always a woman on a mission, and I could see her planning a new one.

When her sobs slackened, she lifted the napkin from her lap and dabbed the black eddies where her makeup had run down her cheeks.

She stared at me with a combination of confusion and the seething fury of a woman scorned.

"How do we nail that bastard's cock to the wall?"

CHAPTER TWENTY-NINE

MALLORY
Marquis Pointe is a five-star resort about an hour north of the city. Even amid the worst pandemic in a generation, couples still retreated there for the exquisite service and stunning views of the mountains. It had all the trappings of the Lodge at Yellowstone Park with the Ritz-Carlton's customer service vibe.

It was the ideal place for an assignation.

It impressed Jillian how quickly Angel composed herself and the speed with which she formulated her plans. Angel met wit with Ted, and they drew up the divorce papers. She handled the family finances and quietly closed their joint investment accounts, splitting the proceeds equally into two checks. Ted helped her with the court paperwork to force Elliot to continue to pay the bills while the spit worked its way through the system.

And my lawyer included another item in the package. A single piece of paper that threatened total exposure of Elliot's misdeeds if he attempted any retribution on me or tried to take my daughter away.

The next time Elliot left for a "business trip," Angel was ready.

When she knew that he and Sherrie were safely ensconced in their room at the Marquis, Angel was in the lobby. The registration was under Sherrie's name. Angel asked the front desk to ring the room on the house phone.

"Hello?"

The youthful voice was breathless.

Angel instantly knew what gymnastics were taking place.

"Sherrie, this is Angel Michaels. Let me talk with my husband."

It wasn't a question. It was a command.

Sherrie stumbled through a half dozen ahs and ums, finally pulling herself together enough to say. "What makes you think he's here?"

Angel's answer was ice cold. "If Elliot is not down in the lobby in two minutes, I will share what I have to show him with every one of his clients, the television stations, and…." she waited to heighten the tension, "your parents."

Two minutes later, Elliot appeared. Angel sat, hands holding the thick file, on one of the Marquis's ostentatious couches.

Elliot's disheveled appearance confirmed what was going on upstairs. "What's this all about, Angel?"

"This folder contains evidence of your affairs with three different women during the course of our marriage. There are also transcripts of videos that show you having sex with your ex-wife, against her will."

Angel lifted a ten-page document off the top of the pile. "This is a separation agreement, the first step toward our divorce. I've cashed out our investment accounts, and there are checks for your half of the money in the folder. I have also changed the locks at our house for my safety. I encourage you to review this information with your attorney and expect you to sign the separation agreement within forty-eight hours, or I'll go public with what I know. And if you—ever—do or say anything to hurt Mallory, even after our divorce is complete, I will spill everything."

Elliot sat stunned and silent. The man who liked control had none for the first time in his life.

Angel stood, dropping the materials into his lap. "Naturally, these are copies. My attorney has the originals. If anything happens to me—He. Will. Destroy. You."

Elliot's soon-to-be ex-wife number two turned and left, seeing the reflection of a broken man in the polished glass of the Marquis's enormous front doors.

CHAPTER THIRTY

ANDREW

Jillian reported Elliot returned the separation agreement the next day. Movers appeared on Monday, and Mallory's ex didn't show up for his promised weekly appointment.

It was time for a celebration.

It surprised me to learn that Jillian had taken Mal under her wing in the kitchen. When Millie and I showed up on Wednesday evening for Mal's "Freedom Party," Jillian's place smelled heavenly.

We gorged on Joule steak and lobster, sautéed spinach, and the best mashed potatoes I've ever tasted. Dessert was a choice of New York-style cheesecake or apple pie. We consumed several bottles of Jillian's favorite Malbec before and during dinner, retreating to her vast living room with our glasses after as Toni handled the clean-up.

Mallory was misty-eyed as she raised a toast. "To the best cook and the most devious bitch on the planet!" She walked over to Jillian and gave her an enormous hug before the two plopped down on the sectional with us and put their feet up on the ottoman.

Millie and I repeated the toast in unison. Jillian bowed. "I'll have to change my professional suffix from MD to DB. But Millie deserves some of the credit. That little 'leave your ex-wife alone' addendum was her work."

"DBI," I joked. "Devious Bitches, Incorporated. I hereby offer my human resource consulting services pro-bono for this new entity."

Jillian was in mid-swallow and choked on her wine. "I'll settle for 'pro-boner.'"

Mille turned to Mal, holding her wineglass in one hand and putting the other on a curvy hip. "You know something, girlfriend? Every woman in this room has known the pleasure of Andrew's measure…. Except me. I'm feeling left out."

"You're feeling horny," Mal shot back. "Red wine does that to you."

"Just looking, and Andrew does that to me," Jillian added, rubbing her crotch and wagging her tongue in my direction. "It's Wednesday night, too. Now that you don't have an ex-husband stalking you, Mallory, how would you feel about sharing the wealth?"

Mal placed her glass on an end table. She pressed one hand down the scoop neck top Jillian wore and fondled a breast, turning Jillian's chin toward her with the other hand.

"Define share," Mallory said. She attacked Jillian's mouth with her own.

The two gave Millie and me quite a performance. Jillian pressed her palms against the sides of Mal's head. She leaned backward on the couch, and my lover climbed on top of her, kissing her mouth with abandon and moving the hand that had been tweaking Jillian's nipple downward until it found the folds of her pantsuit. Exploring fingers found their way to a moistening crotch.

Mal stopped her kissing just long enough to say, "Well! Did you wet your panties, or are you just happy to see me?"

Millie slid next to me and stuck her tongue in my ear. "I can see where this is headed, big boy. Feel like seeing how quickly I can give you an erection?"

This whole business was getting out of hand. "I thought you were working on Eddie?" I asked Mallory's best friend.

"And I'm close to closing the deal, so we had better get to the boinking before I have to be monogamous."

I held out my hands. "Full stop, everyone." All faces looked my way. "I've never had a 'take your boyfriend to work day' with Mallory. I want to see how true professionals serve a customer."

"Only if I can watch," Jillian added before turning her attention back to Mal. "You don't have to stop rubbing my clit, just because some man is trying to run things. They always want to be in charge."

Millie grabbed my hand. "Which way to the master bathroom?"

Jillian and Mal uncoupled, and hand in hand, we four skipped down the hall.

"Hey guys," I giggled. "Can I pee first?"

―――――

MALLORY

Jillian's shower didn't match the massive rainforest experience at Millie's place. But the walk-in was plenty big enough to accommodate all of us. Millie and I worked our magic with Andrew's cock while Jillian swapped spit with such intensity that I felt a tiny pang of jealousy.

We dried our man off before performing our own sensual ballet with towels, purposely focusing on tits and clits with accompanying moans to fully engage Andrew's erection.

But I think we all knew the act was having a similar effect on all of us.

Millie and Jillian each took an arm and escorted Andrew into the bedroom as I followed behind them. I have to admit the sight of three such amazing asses got my juices flowing. I hoped Andrew's acceptance of my sexual diversity would last.

"One request, please," Andrew said as his escorts threw him backward onto the mattress. "No handcuffs tonight. I'm already way outnumbered."

Millie lit up like a flashlight. "You've got handcuffs?"

"Geeze, Millie," Mallory said. "Is there any kink you haven't tried?"

Millie squeezed an ass cheek, shaking her head. "Let's say that there are some that I like less than others. For example, I charge extra for rear entry. That's like prepping for a butt scope. Not fun for the recipient."

Jillian draped an arm around Millie's shoulder, pinching one of her nipples. "When they go home, do you wanna spend the night? I've got some fun toys we could play with."

Jillian's very full implants had Millie's attention. "Ya know, Dr. J, if you put too much saline in those things, they'll bust."

Jillian grinned, sliding an arm under her amplified endowments. "These are extra heavy duty. I'm on the company's beta test team."

This whole interchange bemused Andrew.

"Will you ladies quit fucking around so we can start fucking around?"

Millie gave me the eye, nodding at Jillian's tits. We positioned the doctor at the end of the bed, facing our man, and worked on those over-filled implants. It took moments to figure out that her areola were full-on erogenous zones. Jillian's legs quivered as we began with light young swirls, working inward from the brown edges and tickling the tips of her nipples. She slipped a pair of fingers inside of her opening and massaged her clit with her thumb.

"Good God," she moaned as she tried to focus on Andrew. "If this is doing half as much for you as it is for me, you won't last very long."

"There are some downsides to being a woman," Millie said, between what had grown from light tongue play into full-on tit sucking. "But multiple orgasms isn't one of 'em." She surrounded Jillian's orb with her hands and pulled three more lusty, noisy sucks. "Where is your toy box, Dr. J?"

Jillian could barely get out the words. "By the window."

"Magic wands for everyone!" Millie shouted. "You two have at Mr. Wonderful."

I needed no more encouragement. I bounded onto the mattress and mounted Andrew, slowly sliding him inside of me. The press of his cock against the walls of my pussy was heaven on earth.

Although I had now had sex with a couple dozen different partners, the sensation with this man was the best. I realized that the emotional bond we shared heightened the joy of intercourse way beyond pure physical contact.

I could sense Millie's recognition of my feelings as they wandered back from Jillian's toy box with three creatively crafted dildos in hand. Her face was a wistful tapestry of admiration and envy. Perhaps she had learned that what she wanted was what I had found; that her profession was in pursuit of something she could never attain in a transaction that began with a credit card and ended when the countdown timer hit zero.

Jillian must have felt it, too. I could feel her studying the eye contact between Andrew and me. She took a baton from Millie, pressing the power button and murmuring, "We better make the most of this. Tonight turns a page."

These two amazing women who had so affected my life stood side by side, vibrators pressed against their clits, two voyeurs witnessing genuine love blooming before them.

"I'm losing the best escort in town," Millie muttered before her electronic French tickler found its target.

"But what a ride," Jillian added.

She studied Millie's curves with renewed interest, running her fingers along the contours with tender precision. "I'd love for you to stay," she whispered.

Millie smiled. The two exchanged a brief but meaningful kiss. "I'm a professional. So don't feel too bad if you can't keep up."

CHAPTER THIRTY-ONE

NDREW

Mal recounted that exchange for me later. At the moment, she was the only one I could see. Her moans and the delicious wet rubbing sounds of her grind were all I could hear.

"I love you," she silently mouthed.

"I love you back," I whispered in return.

Mallory's eyes closed. She slowly tilted her head back, increasing her rhythm. I responded by arching to meet her presses until she finally stopped and hovered just above me as my own upward thrusts provided the friction that took us home.

I could feel her walls shudder in orgasm. But it was the satisfied smile on her face that put me over the top. I grabbed her hips and pulled her against me as my spurts filled her.

Mallory collapsed into my arms, and we held one another.

"Dammit," Millie groaned. "She's ruined him for the night."

I stole a glance at Mal's best friend and winked. "The night is just beginning."

———

MALLORY

In that moment, my esteem for my man jumped up another notch. It sounds so counter-intuitive, but I couldn't wait for him to fuck my two friends.

"Who wants a taste," I shouted, rolling onto my back. "One of you suck him spotless." I spread my legs and pointed to my dripping pussy. "The other can get enjoy desert over here."

Jillian pushed Millie toward Andrew. "You're the only one of us who hasn't had this guy yet. Go show him how the pros do it."

Millie grinned and bounced onto the mattress, taking Andrew's softening member into her mouth and performing world-class oral sex on my man until his cock was throbbing again to the point of pain.

Jillian surprised the hell out of me. "I aced every anatomy class in med school," she said as she began slow slurps of the pulsating lips on either side of my opening. "This entire region is one big G-spot. Too many men never learn that lesson."

Her tongue was heavenly. Tender, yet titillating. The visual of her augmented tits swinging back and forth as she worked reminded me that my attraction to the beauty of both men and women would be a dimension of my sexuality for a lifetime.

When she had my labia pulsing in anticipation, she worked her way toward my clit. The light brush of her tongue against the tip sent electrical impulses through my entire body.

"We get more sensitive after each round," Jillian said, taking my pearl into her lips and gently sucking it. "It takes less than half the stimulation to generate the same sensation."

Millie bent back on her knees, her hands on her ample hips as she admired her work. Andrew was again ready for action.

"I hear you have the tongue of a porn star," she said, half challenging, half in mirth. "Want to show it to me?"

Andrew sat up, spinning Millie to the side of the bed with his legs. He picked her up as if she were light as a feather and deposited her on an overstuffed chair near the corner of the bedroom. He took a thigh in each hand, raising and spreading Millie's legs in a single move, pulling her pussy toward his waiting mouth.

"Now, what was Jillian saying about this being one big G-spot?"

Millie jammed her vibrating dildo against her clit. "Just shove that tongue as deep inside of me as you can and start dancing."

Andrew let her spin her fingers against an enormous pearl, but he had his own plans for pleasure, kissing her thighs as she almost begged him to tongue fuck her. Andrew slid closer, working the outer edges of her opening, pausing to suck on her labia when he found a sensitive nerve ending.

When he finally delved inside her, I knew from experience that he could bend that amazing muscle upward until he found the exact point where Millie would be most sensitive.

She pressed the vibrator harder against her clit as Andrew worked his magic, that beautiful tongue sweeping her G-spot again and again until Millie could stand it no longer.

She dropped the toy, threaded her fingers behind her neck, and screamed in ecstasy.

Jillian paused her explorations, and we both watched her vibrating like a windvane in a tornado.

"I've. Never. Felt. Like. That. Before." Millie panted between gasps.

"Okay, pro," Andrew challenged, picking my friend up and tossing her next to us on her back. "I heard you bragging to Jillian about stamina. Let's see what you've got."

He turned to the two of us, pointing to Millie's tits. "Some assistance, please?"

We bounded over, positioning ourselves on either side of Millie's jiggling chest. Andrew threw her knees over his shoulders, slowly pressing his thick cock inside of her.

"Go!" he commanded.

Jillian and I each took a breast in hand, palpating it as we pulled at Millie's enormous nipples with our lips.

"Bring those fingers back down here," he ordered.

Millie, still reeling from her climax on the chair, did so, rubbing her clit between two fingers as Andrew began his thrusts. Then, with his arms around the base of her thighs, he pulled her against him, pressing his cock into her tingling pussy until his pace was almost as fast as her elevated heart rate.

With her head thrust back on a pillow, Millie's mouth opened wide, sucking in oxygen between a crescendo of groans in time with his lightning speed. The friction must have been incredible, but Andrew knew he was working with an instrument that had the capacity. But, like an automotive engineer, he seemed determined to press its limits.

Finally, Millie could no longer control herself. Her hands fell away from her pussy. We unlatched from her tits, and Millie came again, stronger, deeper, and harder than before.

Andrew told me later that her orgasmic clinch felt like a vice. Then, with one last press, he held himself deep inside of her. Millie inhaled a lungful of air and screamed so loud, I thought that the neighbors three doors down might hear her.

Tears streamed down Millie's face. She wilted into whimpering sobs. That surprised Andrew. He gently withdrew, lowered her legs, and balanced above her face, steadying himself with hands placed on either side of her head.

"Are you okay, Mils?" he asked, concern painting his face as droplets of sweat rolled down off of his nose.

Millie nodded and continued to weep, explaining between stuttering inhalations. "I never knew," she said. "I never knew it could feel like this." Millie turned to look at me. "I'm not stealing your man, girlfriend. I promise." Then she looked at Jillian. "So many feelings at once, Jill. Joy and sadness. Gratitude and loss. Hope and despair. A lifetime compressed into a nanosecond."

Jillian gently brushed Millie's hair backward and nodded. "For a moment, you could see clearly, Millie. Do you know what you want now?"

Millie closed her eyes. "Yes. But how will I ever find it?"

Jillian eyed Andrew and me. "Now that you're ready. It will find you."

"I'll get her some water," Andrew said, dismounting my best friend. I held up a hand.

"Let me take her," I said. "You and Jillian have some unfinished business."

CHAPTER THIRTY-TWO

ANDREW

Jillian and I sat alone, facing one another on the bed. Millie's tiny sobs were still audible in the living room, and we could hear Mal's comforting words. Two best friends navigating enlightenment together.

I ran a finger across the top of Jillian's hand. "Thank you. I have a feeling that none of this would have happened if you hadn't been there for that spider bite."

"You're an amazing man, Andrew. I could fall in love with you and never be disappointed."

I chuckled. "Oh, yes, you would. And you know it."

She nodded toward the living room. "For moments like that, I could learn to live with disappointment."

"I need another drink. Something tells me I've got a long night ahead with a soon-to-be ex-sex worker."

I smiled in empathy. "Me, too." I circled her lips with an index finger. "But let's give them their quality time. Got any thoughts on what we might do to keep from getting bored?"

Jillian raised an eyebrow. "I've got a set of handcuffs in that toy box."

I whistled. "This time, you wear 'em. I want to see what it feels like to fuck you with a pair of beach balls bouncing on your chest."

"I overdid it, huh?"

"There was never anything wrong with that body, Jillian. It's yours to play with. But from that first night, it was that beautiful mind that made me hard."

Just saying it refilled my cock. Sweet pain. But pain nonetheless.

Jillian must have seen me wince. "Let me get us both some Advil. Jesus, we sound like old married people."

"I've read that assisted living facilities have the highest STD rates in the nation," I called after her.

When she returned with water and drugs, Jillian's gaze drifted toward the window and the full moon that illuminated the yard. "I wish. I'm worried about something more fundamental. I've been on birth control the whole time we've been fucking one another's lights out. And guess what?"

Jillian patted her belly. "I'm late. Two fucking weeks late."

It took a moment to process the revelation. But for some reason, the news did not upset me. I had my own little epiphany tonight, too. Trust the universe.

"Does Mal know?"

"Of course, she does. She's as giddy as a kid on Christmas morning."

I regarded my fuck buddy. Her aura was different. She was suddenly the definition of beauty. I could feel my attraction transforming from passion to protection.

"So, madame, 'I control my destiny,' what are you thinking? Adoption? Abortion?"

Jillian caressed my face. "I'm thinking 'family.'"

I bent forward until my lips brushed against hers. "Well, I can tell you that the kid's father is delighted. I can get you great rates on teenaged babysitters."

Jillian touched my upper lip with the tip of her tongue. "Why do you have to be so fucking awesome all the time."

"Oh, I'm not. Mal's getting damaged goods. Just ask my girls."

"So you're going to do it?"

"Do what?"

"Marry Mallory?"

I nodded. "Yeah. Are you okay with that? I'm a pretty monogamous guy when I say, 'I do.' Your Wednesdays are going to be a little lonely from now on."

Her hands were grasping the back of my neck. "You taught me something, Andrew," Jillian said as she dragged me on top of her. "Sometimes not getting what you want ultimately gets you what you need."

"One more for the road?" I said, sliding my cock toward her waiting warmth.

Jillian moaned as I entered her. "At least."

CHAPTER THIRTY-THREE

M ALLORY

"It will find you."

I should have known that Millie would never let anything find her.

Two days later, she was banging on my door at seven in the morning, a wicked grin plastered across her face.

"Glad you're up," she said, ignoring my barely open eyes. "I'm so keyed-up and have to tell somebody."

My BFF pushed past me and made a beeline for the living room.

"The kid's still sleeping," I whispered. "Please keep the theatrics on low volume."

From here, I'll let her tell the story.

That night with Andrew changed everything. I spent the whole next day processing what happened. I wondered if my little miss confidence act was a shield I was throwing up between Eddie and me.

Was he the guy I was looking for all along?

Yeah, I know that look, Mal. You think I'm nuts.

Well, I am, and so is that skinny little shit. So I got out my Post-it notes and started making a list of all our strengths and weaknesses. Strengths on the green ones and weaknesses on the red ones.

Dammit to hell. They almost all complement each other. Isn't that how love works? You share the basics in common, values, physical attraction, that stuff. And the rest are complementary. You know, the Jerry Maguire, "You Complete Me" thing.

Why wouldn't Eddie and I be a perfect fit?

Well, one of my greens is that I'm a dog with a bone when I latch on to an idea. And one of Ed's reds is that he can't concentrate on something for more than a minute.

I decide that we are going to work. We're going to have the most amazing, outlandish, unpredictable love that any two people have ever had.

When that's your truth, you don't wait another minute to live it.

So I ping his admin. He's due back from LA late, like eleven something. I talk my way into his house and convince his security guys that I'm supposed to pick him up at the airport in the McLaren!

They fucking buy it! Moments later, I'm driving this half-million-dollar car to meet a private jet with my man in it.

I convince the cops at the executive terminal to let me drive right up to the plane after it lands. I pop open the passenger door as Eddie walked down the gangplank and yell, "Get in, handsome."

He's so clueless that he thinks he asked me to come to get him and just forgot.

I plant a kiss the size of the Empire State Building on his mouth and peel out.

"Listen, Eddie," I say. "You're the craziest guy I've ever known, and I know I'm the craziest girl you've ever met. I don't care about your crazy hours, your ADD brain, and your

addiction to entrepreneurship. You can forget our dates. You can answer the phone in the middle of our fuck-fests. You can do whatever you want. But I'm always going to be the one person you can count on to be there for you when you need me."

Ed is slack jawed. He can't believe what's happening.

"Let's be honest, Eddie," I say. "There's probably not another woman on the planet who can put up with you, let alone love you. But I can and I will, for better or worse, for richer or poorer, as long as we both shall live."

His cell is ringing, but he's so stunned he doesn't even hear it. "That sounds like a marriage proposal," he finally stutters.

"It is," I say. "And we're on the way to a justice of the peace to make it official before you start focusing on some new idea or the next big deal."

He stumbles through a long sentence of unintelligible monosyllables.

"I'm not after your money, and here's the prenup to prove it. You can dump me anytime, and I'll walk out of your life with the same net worth I had when I walked into it. But I promise you that nobody will ever love you more deeply, support you with greater intention, or believe in you, no matter how the chips fall. You're marrying my fat ass, Edward, and you're doing it tonight."

I skid to a stop in front of this dimly lit house in the middle of nowhere with a "Justice of the Peace - Notary Public" sign on the mailbox. And drag him by the hand toward the front door.

"I haven't read the prenup," he stutters. "And don't I need a best man?"

"Your lawyers have read it, and we'll do something more church-like later if you want."

I pound on the door, and this dude opens it in his pajamas.

"We're here to get married," I say, pressing the license I got earlier in the day at the courthouse into his face, along with five one-hundred-dollar bills.

The guy is stunned until he counts the cash and says, "Come on in."

Before Eddie knows it, this bearded dairy farmer and part-time public servant is asking us the marriage questions. His bleary-eyed wife and two neighbors are witnessing.

And dammit if Eddie doesn't answer every one with "I will."

Moments later, I'm sucking his face and we're headed to his place, where I channel every emotion I felt with you and Andrew in Eddie's direction. Jesus, the sex was fantastic. Three hours, non-stop.

This morning at six, he rolls out of bed and says two things. "I've got to get on a conference call," and "I guess we should go to the jewelry store so you can pick out a ring."

"Holy shit," was all I could say. And I said it loud enough to wake up Ella.

Millie exhales. "So I'm married for the second time, Mal. The coast is clear. Go nail Andrew's feet to the matrimonial floor. I'll be super pissed if you let Jillian grab him first."

CHAPTER THIRTY-FOUR

ANDREW
Within a month, Mal put her house on the market and moved in with me. This elated Dana and Dani. And it surprised me when I saw Patty's caller ID on my cell.

"Hey, Andy." Her voice was breezy, and I could tell she wanted something. "The girls are getting to that age where they could benefit from more time with their biological dad. So I'm okay with us changing the terms of the divorce decree where they can spend as much time as they want with you."

I couldn't keep the sarcasm totally out of my answer. "Great. So puberty comes and you are okay passing off two hormonal crazies to someone else?"

Patty cackled like she always did when I caught her playing games. "Well…to be totally honest, they are driving Phil up a wall. He has a chance to take a relo to the coast and pulling the girls out of school so close to graduation doesn't feel like a good idea. If you're okay with full custody, I'll sign the papers."

"You can have them whenever you want them," I said. "You'll always be their mother. And who knows? Someday they may want marital advice from you."

I could tell Patty felt the dig. She shrugged it off. "I'm no prize, Andy. You know that, and Phil knows it, too. We're struggling, and I'm hoping a new location with just us two will give us a chance for a fresh start."

I could feel Patty's pain and truly wanted to wish her well. "I hope things work out for you and Phil, Patty. I'll always be grateful that you and I created Dana and Dani. May you find the happiness you seek."

———

"SHE'S CHEATED ONCE. SHE'LL CHEAT AGAIN." THE knowing smile I predicted spread across my psychiatrist's face at our next appointment. "It's only a matter of time."

She closed her notebook and locked me in another of those stares that meant she was about to give me direction.

"Just how many women are you sleeping with these days."

She could see the embarrassment on my face. "Just one. But my record is three at once."

"You may have taken my advice about extraordinary passion during extraordinary times a little further than I would have recommended, but if all involved are okay with the situation, let it be."

I blushed. "I've asked Mal to marry me."

"Who couldn't see that one coming a mile away? What do Jillian and Millie think about it?"

"Why would that matter?"

My shrink closed her eyes as I imagined she did when explaining something super simple to a simpleton. "Mallory has discovered an additional dimension of her sexuality with Millie and has a much longer history with her. So be prepared for those two to continue to romp together in the bedroom."

"I'm not demanding that Mal give up anything about her life or career," I said, meaning every word. "If Millie and a procession of other male clients are part of that life, I will have to live with it."

"Easier said than done," my shrink countered. "What about Jillian?"

"What about Jillian?" I returned.

"Will you two continue your Wednesday night madness?"

"She and Mal have become buddies," I said. "I'll leave that decision up to the two of them. There are complications."

My shrink sat back in her chair, tapping her pen on the notepad with my name on it. "I'm listening."

"Jillian is pregnant. She and Mal are over the moon about it. It feels like we may become an unconventional family."

My psychiatrist stood, looking at the "times up" clock on the wall.

"Just remember. The human heart is the only thing more vexing than the human mind. And, as the old Yiddish saying goes, 'An erection makes you bury your brains in the dirt.'"

The woman who had kept me centered through every twist and turn gave me a hug.

"Life is a series of negotiations. Our needs evolve as we learn and grow. Don't be afraid to re-negotiate when necessary."

———

MALLORY

For reasons I still can't fathom, Millie and Ed clicked. She didn't make demands. That alone seemed to rein him in. She embarrassed him at parties with the same act she pulled at the Maracaibo and he loved every minute. They set up a non-profit to support sex workers and legalize recreational marijuana. And as the pandemic loosened its grip, Ed's business roared back. We brought the staff back online, and my boss actually spent two weeks with my best friend, his new wife, in Bermuda.

She still won't tell me what they did.

———

I SHOULD HAVE KNOWN WHAT ANDREW WAS UP TO when he suggested a family outing on a Wednesday night, the night he was usually with Jillian.

By now, things were opening up again, and we took Ella with us to The Rail Yard Chop House, the city's most expensive and exclusive restaurant. He reserved the 20th Century Limited Room, a tiny alcove with a view of the city.

When the best steak dinner I ever had began to digest, Andrew turned to Ella.

"We have something for Mommy, don't we?"

On cue. Ella reached into her pocket and pulled out a tiny blue box. And I knew.

Andrew dropped to a knee, facing the two of us.

"Mallory and Ella Michaels, will you accept me as a husband and a father? Will you help me build a family we can all be proud of? Will you endure all of my flaws and let me love you with all of my heart?"

He turned to focus on me. I was already a teary-eyed mess.

"Mallory. Will you honor me by being my soulmate, my life partner, and my wife for as long as we both shall live?"

I could. I would. And I did say "Yes."

Then Andrew turned his loving gaze to my miracle girl.

"Ella, will you let me become your father? Will you allow me to love you as much as I love Dana and Dani? Will you give me the honor of being there for you during every twist and turn of your life's adventures, supporting you with my heart and the fruits of my labor, for as long as I live?"

The stinker must have rehearsed this with my kid without my knowledge. She threw her arms around his neck, kissing his cheek and saying the one word that symbolized what I never thought I could ever provide for her again.

"Daddy!"

CHAPTER THIRTY-FIVE

MALLORY
How do you hold a wedding in the middle of a pandemic?

Andrew and I made it an "immediate family" event. And our definition only included our kids. Millie was my maid of honor. Ed was Andrew's best man. A very pregnant Dr. Jillian Walcott was the witness.

We did the deed at City Hall. I was a little nervous to see so many familiar faces there who were "Donna" and "Gina's" clients. Our blended trio of children bonded. Dani applied to colleges with special education majors, and Ella's vocabulary blossomed with two more teachers drilling her every day. But in a time where every event happened on Zoom, those who still made the trek downtown seemed glad to have something happy to celebrate.

With my new situation, I didn't need the extra cash. And in our work-at-home world, Andrew and I could do the mating dance whenever we wanted. I continued to have occasional dinners with former clients. But my days of thousand-dollars-per-hour passion were over.

Amber, my babysitter, agreed to keep Ella for the wedding weekend, and Dani and Dana reluctantly masked up and boarded an airplane for a visit to their mom and stepdad's new home on the coast.

Of course, Ed had work to do.

That left just us four to figure out how to commemorate the monumental day.

Jillian cooked. It was an Italian extravaganza—ziti, chicken picatta, meat lasagna, the best Italian salad I had ever eaten, and several bottles of the most incredible wine I've ever tasted.

Millie baked us a tiny wedding cake—strawberry with white cream cheese frosting. Somewhere she found a perverted topper, a bride bending over with her white gown pulled up and the groom glued to her ass with a smile on his face. Two other characters completed the cake-top tableau, a pair of women sitting in chairs, watching the proceedings with tiny wax vibrators pressed between their legs.

Jillian, the witness/voyeur, took the requisite cake-cutting photographs of me shoving a slice into Andrew's mouth, followed by a photo of me snowballing it back into my own.

"You gotta work on your technique," Jillian yelled as she and Millie squealed with delight.

Then it was time for the toasts.

Millie stood first, more than a little tipsy from the wine.

"I've known the bride since we were thirteen years old. We've shared everything." She gave Andrew a look when she said the word, repeating it so he'd know the full meaning. "*Everything*, Andrew. And I can see what he likes about her. Not only is she a wonderful human and a great mother, but she's the best fuck I ever had." Millie nodded to Jillian. "And I've had every possible fuck there is to have."

"Thank you, Millie," I said, trying to get her to shut up and sit down. "I love you, too."

She turned to my newly minted husband. "Andrew," Millie's eyes grew wet. "Not only were you the most memorable one-night stand of my life..." Her voice cracked. "Thank you for showing me the way."

Andrew stood and embraced my best friend. "You knew it all along, Millie. Now go chase it."

I thought about how lucky I felt, about how our ups and downs turned out to have happy endings, about the amazing people who transformed my life, and the unknown that lay ahead for all of us.

I raised my glass. "I love you all. Here's to family and the future. May our bonds become stronger and every adventure bring us closer."

"Oh shit!"

Jillian rolled her eyes, leaning against the island in Andrew's kitchen, her nine-month baby belly distended like a beached whale.

"What?" I said. "I think emotional moments are super sweet, Jillian."

"It's not that," she said, crossing her arms on top of the new life that grew inside of her. "My water just broke."

ACKNOWLEDGMENTS

"Who writes stuff like this," my mother said seconds before my brother outted me as an author of romantic fiction.

She was at first appalled, until I reminded her that stories I sold during my college years paid the bills.

Then, she made a surprising admission. For the last 10 years of my grandmother's life, she was, herself, a prolific author of short, steamy romance stories. She figured out how to get them on Smashwords and made enough money to buy us all very expensive Christmas presents and finance her annual cruise adventures.

And we thought grandpa left her a fortune!

I first learned that I might be able to earn a living in this space from my college guidance counselor, a man, who funded his technology addiction with short smut. And yes, I did pay for much of my college experience with the proceeds of my writing.

The creative process is a community effort. My family includes the awesome Stephie Walls who edits my stuff. Robin Harper creates my covers. And I'm grateful to the beta readers who checked my facts and shared their wisdom.

My spouse and family don't always understand what I do. But we are all grateful for the opportunities The Craft provides. I could not create without their love and support.

Most of all, thank YOU for reading Pandemic Love. I hope it left you in a better place than you were before. Love is Love. There's not nearly enough of it in the world.

May we all spread it around!

MacKenzie Masters
Seattle, Washington
Summer 2021

ABOUT MACKENZIE

MacKenzie Masters loves writing delectably steamy stories. Her earliest romantic fiction earned accolades from her fifth grade classmates and a disciplinary trip to the principal's office. She's been creating steamy love stories ever since, from her home base in Seattle, Washington.

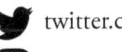 twitter.com/MackenzieMast86
 instagram.com/mackenziemasters

Please Her

A chance encounter with a beautiful woman begins a 5 year journey of discovery for a 21-year-old orphan and his 33-year-old mentor. Both navigate life's twists and turns. Both want to find the right soulmate for the other, not realizing that perhaps the unique relationship they share is the true love they have both been wishing for all along.

Follow Mack at MackenzieMasters.com.